Undertaken and Undone

Undone Series, Volume 3

K.R. Cook

Published by K.R. Cook, 2022.

---

1. http://www.authorkrcook.com

Also by K.R. Cook

Submerged Series
Submerged
Unleashed
Overcoming

Undone Series
Undead and Undone
Untamed and Undone
Undertaken and Undone
Unleashed and Undone
Undeniable and Undone

Watch for more at https://www.authorkrcook.com/.

Table of Contents

Notes and Triggers:

This book is not a dark romance. Sex scenes are detailed and consensual. That being said, there are themes some may find triggering:

- Detailed sex scenes (consensual)
- Mention of past torture
- Mention of past murder, including being drained by a vampire and/or killing a vampire to escape (deserved)
- Fist fight
- Discrimination based on vampire status
- Attempted sexual assault (don't worry – Julian rescues Ivy)
- Biting against one's will (werewolves bite Ivy)
- Hearts being ripped out of werewolves (deserved)
- Séance performed: speaking with the dead, demon attack (unseen force leaves one gasping for air and panicking)
- Mention of polygamy and sexual abuse of a minor (Julian, when he was on the run at sixteen and lived with a polygamous werewolf pack)
- Stabbing someone with a crowbar (they live)
- A fight, including neck stabbing, choking, drenched in aconite, blood
- Murder victims found (don't want to spoil too much with a location)
- Vomiting blood
- Dark magick being used, including using a dagger to bleed for spell and unleashing a demon (accidentally)
- Possession and attempted murder

Cover made using Canva.

Chapter 1. A Vampire and a Werewolf

I saw him at Vudu for the first time, the wolf. The werewolf.

Julian Napper.

Seeing a werewolf in a club populated by vampires and humans was odd to me. But watching him dance in leather pants, his bare chest exposed and full of rippling muscles as he awkwardly moved against that shiny silver pole, was anything but odd.

In fact, it'd filled me with an undeniable urge to touch those muscles, to run my hands along his strong chest, to feel the soft brunette hairs there and the bumps of his bulging abs that covered his stomach. I'd never wanted to touch someone so badly before, to kiss them and mold myself to them. And I hadn't been touched in decades. My body yearned for him to run his hands all over it, to expel the throb between my thighs.

It was demanding, really, the pull I felt toward him, the *need* to feel him, to have him... as my own.

Seeing all those women ogle him at Vudu had left the cool blood slowly moving through my vampiric veins nearly boiling with jealousy. I'd wanted to blind all of them with my own nails like a mad crow scratching at their eyes, but there really was no need. His focus wasn't on them; his gaze was direct, unrelenting, on *me*.

That was the night I'd met up with my friend Derick at the infamous vampire club to discuss taking down the High Society, an evil and powerful vampire organization the two of us were part of... one we both wanted to destroy. Derick hadn't just brought his lover, Hailey, along. To spy on me, they'd dressed Julian up as a Vudu stripper in an attempt to keep an eye out for trouble, to ensure *I* wasn't the traitor who'd not only outed Julian's pack for helping to end the High Society, but also Derick for planning the same, all of which resulted in the two of them being tortured for a day and Julian's pack being slaughtered right in front of him. Turns out, Julian had a traitor in his pack (Denise), and Derick hadn't considered the fact that the High Society was spying on he and I all along, having planted cameras all over our apartments and in our vehicles.

Catherine, the leader of the High Society and Jerry, her foolish sidekick, were responsible for their torture, and I wanted to kill them both for not only hurting my longtime friend Derick, but for touching Julian... a wolf whose broken spirit called out to my own, seeking to pull me into his world.

Since that moment, I want to believe that he feels that same pull, the one that still beckons me to him... but since meeting Julian, he's always shown... restraint. Even when we'd been hiding out together for days, just the two of us, from the High Society, he hadn't made a move. Not that I did either, not then anyway. Lately, I've flirted and hinted at what I want – him. Flirting's one thing. Begging is another. I got over begging for anything after I was turned into a vampire.

I once begged along the streets of Chicago for pennies and food in the nineteen-thirties, before I was found by a vampire who wanted me as his vampire bride. He'd preyed on me until the moment he gave me his blood against my will and drained me. "Ivy," he'd purred between bites. "Such a beautiful name, indeed, for a stunning Greek goddess like yourself. But not quite as beautiful as something more delicate... like Rose. Yes, Rose. That's your name now, my delicate flower." As he drained me, I'd grown weaker, colder... and darkness had soon claimed me. I'd awakened in his upscale home in a richer area of my beloved city. But I'd refused to be his bride and killed him just before he'd vowed to force my hand. That's when the High Society had found me and offered me comfort and safety in exchange for my help in cleaning up the streets of Blumhaven, Texas, disposing of evidence left behind from careless vamps on a feeding frenzy.

When I joined the High Society, we executed such murderous monsters after clearing out the bodies the vamps left behind. But as the decades wore on, the organization had given into their own urges and began mutilations of their own. I'd eventually seen them for what they were, or rather, what they'd become: selfish, evil fiends who needed to be taken down. Derick Shaw, a friend and member of the High Society as I was, agreed with me. He too saw their evil ways. But he had his own set of rules he intended to follow to eliminate them. While he acted more impulsively (especially when he met his fiancé Hailey and vowed to protect her from them), I was more calculated and careful. I never understood how he could let his guard down so easily with Hailey... not until I met Julian.

Now I get it. I think about him far too often when he's not around... and when he is around, my focus is even worse off.

I just know, whether he does or not, that we're made for each other. We're meant to be. But what exactly does that mean, being meant for someone? To a vampire, it means forever, deciding to be with someone you deem a soulmate. To a wolf, finding their mate in life means they're bound to that person by some kind of magic... whether they want to be or not (but from what I know, they *do* want it... once they meet them).

I'd like to believe I'm Julian's mate because of this undeniable pull I feel to him. But if I am, could he really deny me so easily? With only vengeance driving him these days, would he even notice anything else?

Since Julian isn't making any moves or indicating that he feels as strongly for me as I do for him, I've decided I'm not his mate. It'd be silly anyway, wouldn't it? A vampire being with a werewolf? One might think so, but they might not know the story of Madison and Dorian, new friends of mine with whom I adore, who are mates. Madison wasn't always a wolf. She'd been turned into a vampire by a serial killer, one Julian and I are currently hunting on the side. Our primary focus is on Denise, though... the *"wolf bitch"* who used to be in Julian's pack but handed him and everyone else over to the High Society. But back to Madison. She'd bitten that vampire serial killer's hand the night he'd attacked her, taking in his blood, before he'd snapped her neck in a moment of panic upon being discovered by Dorian in the alleyway he'd summoned her to. He'd taken her there to drain her and dispose of her like he's been doing with other girls lately... other blondes. Dorian had taken Madison in and taken care of her, showing her the ropes of being a vamp (before she was made wolf by him, her mate). They've been together since. They even just had a baby, a beautiful girl named Allison, but we call her Allie. Who knew wolves could have babies in two months?! Even werewolves, apparently... and Allie's growing quickly.

They share a bond, Madison and Dorian... that magical mate bond. When he'd bitten her just to see what would happen (Madison had a feeling she'd turn if he did), she transitioned. She went from running room temp and possessing no beating heart to having a heart that pumped hot blood through her veins and gave her a warmer touch. There was never a risk in biting her... a wolf bite doesn't kill us vamps. It just hurts like hell. She was always meant to be his... his wolf mate.

But me?

I'm not meant to be Julian's. If I were, he'd want me back.

Wouldn't he?

Sure, he cares about me. I've seen it. Like when I'd once gotten sick from not feeding for too long when we'd been hunting the High Society. He'd carried me to a blood bank, going as far as breaking in and stealing bags for me. He'd cared for me that night.

Just being around him... I've never felt so... alive before.

I've also seen him jealous, or at least that's what it'd seemed like when he'd asked me if I'd ever fed off men before. Sure I have. They're usually more willing than women to go off into a dark corner with me. But I've always fed out of hunger, not because I'd desired them.

Now Julian, on the other hand... I want to sink my teeth into him and ride him all night long.

Question is: Does he want me to?

Chapter 2. Marv's

The sex shop I manage – Vixen – is open from six at night till two in the morning, seven days a week. It sits along a strip in the bustling city of Blumhaven, Texas. Since Derick and Dorian took over Club Vudu, which is not far from Vixen, I've been here, keeping the shop open and operating like normal. We sell lingerie, a ridiculous selection of lubricants, toys, videos, edibles, condoms (the flavored strawberry ones are popular) and the promise of seduction and sex.

Being a vampire, I naturally give off a seductive allure. My mesmerizing amber irises never fail me, my gaze sensual and flirtatious as I stare directly at my intended prey (ahem, customer). I've often batted my thick black lashes at customers while playfully twirling the long, shiny, wavy, voluminous black strands of my hair around my alabaster fingers, enrapturing them as I recommend products with seduction in my tone. At five-foot-four, my frame petite, I often add to my height by wearing boots or Mary Janes at least three-inches tall. Short leather skirts with Vixen tees or waist-defined dresses are my go-to, though I do sometimes wear a nice, tight pair of black jeans. My hips are much wider than my waist, and my shoulders and breasts are small. A true pear-shape, I am. Wandering eyes have often left mine to linger at my chest, hips and bare legs. In working at a sex shop such as this one, I've become accustomed to such attention, deciding to use my appeal to garner success for the store. Lately, I've even delighted more than usual in the appreciation customers have shown me, their desire for me obvious in their dilating pupils or the way they lean toward me... since I'm not getting that sort of attention from Julian.

He's always all about business. We've been searching for Denise and a serial killer vampire (the same who who'd tried to kill Madison). Even when I've worn the shortest of skirts, running the tips of my fingers delicately over my thighs in front of him, he's stayed focused on paperwork, phone calls, even boring old maps! There's so much tension built up in those massive shoulders of his, that even my massages haven't loosened them. If anything, he's become stiffer under my touch (and not in the good way). He's even excused himself from the room before, giving the excuse of needing to use the restroom, make a call or get some air. He's abnormally obsessed with finding Denise, the traitor who'd led the High Society to his pack and got them all killed, his sight so profoundly blinded by revenge, that he hasn't made any time to have sex with me. Perhaps I've been too passive aggressive. Shall I crawl onto his lap and plant my lips on his soon? Straddle him in one of those wooden chairs he often sits upon in his kitchen while he studies clues scattered about his cluttered table? How I wish he'd lift me onto that table and settle himself between my thighs...

I blink myself out of that fantasy before I'm driven mad with unrequited passion. I shift my attention from Julian fantasies to the shelf in front of me, grabbing the bottle of lube a customer just asked for. I turn and show the medium-sized translucent grey bottle to her with a smile. "I believe this is what you're looking for."

She flushes scarlet as her widened blue eyes flash to the bottle. "I-I've never used lube before."

"No? Well, it's easy to use, and this one is water-based, which is better for those with allergies to oils."

She tentatively reaches for the bottle and examines it in her hands, which are shaking just so slightly, a movement that would be impossible for any other human to detect. Her heartbeat is loud and fast, pumping blood through her veins. Another thing no one but me notices right now.

"You're nervous," I observe aloud.

She looks at me, the reddened blush across her cheeks deepening, before she glances around the shop, lowering her voice: "I've never had sex before."

She's young, probably twenty-one, the same age I am... in appearance anyway. Judging by the quick heartbeat and shaking fingers... "Are you sure you want to?"

A frown appears. "My boyfriend wants to, and I figure if I want to keep him around, I should do this... to show him how much he means to me."

That sounds like something she's been told. Surely she didn't come to this decision all on her own. A rage begins to build inside me, igniting a fire in my veins, turning the cool trickling fluid room temperature. "Is he pressuring you?"

She shrugs. "No..." I'm not buying it, and soon, as I stare her down, she admits the truth: "Well, maybe sort of."

I look her over, from her perfect, shiny, and straight brown hair to the baby pink cardigan and dark jeans she wears. Her heels are designer, pink like her cardigan. She reminds me of a sorority girl, the popular kind who aims to please others while sacrificing her own happiness and needs. I imagine her boyfriend is tall, buff and has messy light brown hair and a tan from constantly tossing a football in front of the frat house he lives in. He doesn't play football... no, he only wishes he'd been good enough to be on the college team. Instead, he's majoring in business or something equally unlike his desires, per his father's wishes. Having no control over his future, he's practiced control in other areas... such as with the cardigan-wearing virgin standing before me. If this boyfriend of hers were here, I'd frighten him with a simple look, maybe even convince him using my mind control ability to back off and stop pressuring his girlfriend into sex. But he's not here. Lucky for him. Since he isn't, I offer unsolicited advice: "If he doesn't want to wait for you to be ready, I'd dump him."

Her perfectly filled-in brows pull in as she looks at me, a reaction I recognize as defensive. "I didn't ask for your opinion."

Perhaps I've pegged her wrong, and she's not so innocent. "Well," I say, turning around and waltzing to stand behind the register. I focus my soft brown gaze on hers, pulling her mind into my own. "Forget I gave it." I smile much too brightly, resuming the professional act of a seller discussing a product with a customer and nothing more. "Shall I ring you up?"

She looks uncertain, like she wants to leave, her eyes flitting between the counter and the door, but she comes to the counter and buys the lube without another word, not even another glance at me. I don't watch her leave. Her problems aren't my own. I've got bigger fish to fry, like the serial killer vamp I'll be prowling the streets for later. The missing girls have all been around this area, only going as far over as two towns. He's around... somewhere... and I know how to hunt down no-good vamps. Especially ones Madison has described as "skeletal". He won't be hard to spot, not with those prominent cheekbones and all-around dead-like aura. And since he goes for blondes, the brown-haired girl who'd just left is safe... from the vampire, anyway.

At one-thirty in the morning, the shop is empty, and a familiar feeling hits me, one that makes my heart flutter as though I'm human again, even though no beats sound out. Sometimes it feels like it might actually beat... when *he's* around.

The bell above the door dings as Julian walks in, his tall and built frame taking up over half the entrance. As far as looks go, he appears twenty-three-ish, but he's actually much older. Werewolves don't age after they've been turned, just like vamps. Today, he's wearing faded medium-blue jeans, ones that are stained with black oil that's never completely washed out, a hole on the right knee from where they'd once ripped when he'd been fixing his motorcycle. This pair is one of my favorites – they hug his backside just right. His moto boots are just as old as those jeans, the dark leather dusted with dirt, the toes worn. His dark grey cotton tee is tighter around his broad shoulders than his waist, the short sleeves revealing bulging, tan biceps. His dark wavy hair hangs over his thick brows. Those eyes, grey yet blue but also green and filled with golden flecks, meet mine.

My pink, glossed mouth hangs open, dry suddenly (like my throat). He spots me stocking dildos and comes over, barely glancing at the rubber penises contained by plastic in my hands. He's been here many times before, and these items have no affect on him... like me (I'm not bitter or anything about that fact).

"You about ready to head out?" he asks in that deep southern drawl of his, the one that makes my knees turn to Jell-O and stomach quiver as though butterflies are swarming about inside it. "Got a call from a friend that our vamp is at Marv's again. They're gonna try to hold him there till we can make it out."

Finally! A real lead! This vamp we're after has been to Marv's (a werewolf bar in Whispering Creek) once before tonight. He showed up last month, flirted with a blonde, and they'd left together. She was never seen again. The wolves that work there are fully aware of his involvement in recent murders, but they told Julian they'd prefer to stay out of vampire matters so as not to draw the wrong kind of attention to themselves. Instead, they said they'd just call Julian the next time the vamp showed up scouring the place for victims. I hope we make it in time to catch him before he gets another girl.

I quickly hang the plastic cases holding faux penises. "Of course, let's go."

"It ain't two yet. That okay?"

I look around the empty shop. We usually close at two, but with no customers around... "I can close early. This is more important."

"Good, don't wanna miss him."

I don't, either. That evil prick is going to be turned to dust soon enough!

Outside Vixen, parked along the curb, is Julian's new motorcycle. Colored all black and shining under the streetlamp, I bite my bottom lip imagining him riding it, wishing it were me he was riding instead.

What is it with wolves and motorcycles, anyway? Madison's husband (Dorian) has one as well. I spot two helmets hanging off the handlebar, one hot pink, the other black. Did he get that hot pink helmet for me? It *is* my favorite color...

Being a wolf with fast-healing abilities and all, he doesn't really need a helmet... and neither do I, being a vamp and all. But I know that Julian doesn't want to be hassled by cops (even though he is one) trying to determine if he's old enough to be riding without one or has the appropriate medical insurance to get away with not using one.

He picks up the pink helmet and hands it to me. "Put this on."

I take it from him and begin to unfasten the strap. "Get this just for me, did you?"

He puts his own helmet on, blocking my view of his expression. "Figure if we're gonna be ridin' around together, you need one."

But he specifically got a *pink* one...

Does it mean something?

Not wanting to tease him too much, I say no more... but I do ache for his touch. "Help a girl out, would you?" I ask, pretending to be having difficulty with the strap.

He stands in front of me, towering over my petite frame, and grabs the strap from between my fingers, his warm caress sending excited shivers through me, all the way from my dainty fingers to the tips of my onyx-painted toes. From my limp hands, he takes the helmet and puts it over my head, securing the strap under my small chin. Visor still up on my own helmet, my reflection stares back at me from the closed visor on his. Behind that tinted plastic, a bright glow emanates within his eyes, lighting them up like the ocean on a sunny day. I almost hate how he's turned me into a corny, lovesick schoolgirl. I'm supposed to be a fierce vampire, unafraid of the most frightening of monsters... not a whimsical sixteen-year-old with a heart-crippling crush.

Although, this doesn't feel like a crush. It's... deeper than that.

He turns away from me and straddles his bike, patting the seat behind him. "Come on."

At five-four, I climb on behind his six-four frame, delightfully snaking my hands slowly around his sides and settling them against his muscled torso, fingers intertwined for a firmer hold across the cotton tee he wears, the muscles on his abdomen tightening in response. His outer thighs, stationed right between mine, are warm, his jeans rough against the bare skin of my inner thighs. Having worn a mini navy dress today, my pink skull-decorated underwear are right up against his backside, my thighs exposed against him, wishing he'd touch them. But his hands are on the handlebars, not my thighs. ...Unfortunately.

"Glad I didn't wear jeans today," I admit, waiting for his reaction. "I like the feel of you between my bare legs."

Normally, I practice more modest flirting with him, but I've been at a sex shop all day, naturally thinking about sex with him, wondering if he thinks about having it with me, too...

He clears his throat before starting the bike, a rumble from the engine loudly drowning out the sound of his increased heartbeat.

Sometimes I think I *do* affect him, just not as much as I wish. Only a mate could get him in bed, I'm sure. Or perhaps another wolf. After months of flirting, I've gotten nowhere near close to seducing him, which has begun to feel like a task. Something like seduction should come easily for a vamp, and if he were human or vampire, I'd like to think I would've already had him. But he's a wolf... a guarded, vengeful wolf.

Still, I hold him close, wishing he'd want me, fantasizing about that very thing on the drive over to Marv's, imagining him ripping my dress and underwear off and claiming me on his bike like Dorian once did to Madison. I've been living vicariously through her and Hailey lately, hanging off every word as they've shared their steamiest sex stories with me. I squeeze my thighs against his and push my hips against his without thought. How would he *feel*, inside me, holding me close, giving me pleasure while he cocoons me safely against his strong chest, his hips between mine, his...

"We're here," Julian announces.

We'd stopped? I didn't even realize...

I hold onto his broad shoulders to get off his bike, even though I don't need to. Does he know that? After unbuckling the helmet from under my chin and fastening it to his handlebar, I glance at the other bikes in the lot, ones parked in a line like his.

"Wolves and bikes...," I mutter.

Julian gets off his motorcycle and pulls his helmet free, a grin playing on his lips, but he doesn't say anything. At the door, he pauses and grabs my hand, sending a jolt of electricity through me. If I breathed, I'd have gasped and gotten dizzy. How I've longed for him to hold my hand, to secure it within his own protectively, to warm it in more than one way...

He looks down at me, his eyes glowing brighter. "From this point forward, you're mine. Got it?"

Oh, how I wish that were true, but there has to be a reason for him to tell me this now, and it isn't because he actually wants me to be his. ...Is it? "What?"

"Vamps don't often come here. It's safer for you... if they know you're with me."

Ugh, his voice is so deep and sexy and southern. ...But there's the disappointing reason for saying what he'd said, about me being his. It's for my own safety. "Oh... okay."

Looking on the bright side, at least I can pretend for a few that I really am his girlfriend, deluding myself further and probably causing more grief for myself in the future when he inevitably tells me he likes me as a friend. I'm not naturally a glutton for punishment, but this wolf certainly makes it seem so.

Julian opens the door and enters with me, holding my hand safely inside his own still. A few wolves look at us, but they don't approach us. Mostly, it's humans here, save for the bikers taking up several booths against a wall and the workers managing the bar and kitchen.

Heavy metal plays from a juke box, a few dim lights in need of a good dusting hang from the ceiling, and a pool table and dartboard occupy an area to our left. Glass mugs holding amber liquid with foam gathered around the top sit on tables nearest those playing pool and darts, though there are some dark green bottles containing beer as well scattered about the place. The biker wolves occupying the booths seem to prefer the draft rather than the beer already in bottles.

But where's our deadly vamp?

Julian squeezes my hand tighter as he approaches the bar. "Patrick, where's he at?"

The red-headed guy named Patrick slings a dirty rag over his shoulder while he eyes Julian, then his gaze finds mine, his brown eyes widening, his jaw hanging open. "You brought a vamp in here?!"

Julian stiffens, his back becoming straighter. "You got a problem with that?"

Patrick's eyes dart away from mine, his brows furrowing as he looks down at his shoes. "No..."

"All right, then," Julian says gruffly. "Now where's he at?"

Patrick shrugs, eyes still on the floor. "Left a few minutes before you got here."

Julian's voice booms out: "What the fuck, Pat? I said hold him!"

Patrick finally looks at Julian again, holding his hands up as he does. "I tried. I even offered him a beer on the house!"

"Vamps don't drink no fuckin' beer!" Julian growls out.

"Well shit, man." Patrick nods toward me. "I don't follow what vamps do and don't do, unlike you, who clearly bangs 'em."

My eyes widen as much as they possibly can at that comment. If only, dear Patrick! If only!

Julian's grip on my hand tightens again, just before he uses his other to jab a thick finger toward Patrick. "Watch your mouth."

Patrick is clearly younger in wolf years than Julian. I know this by what he says next, a statement no one should ever challenge someone like Julian with: "Or what?"

A vein in Julian's neck moves thickly against the skin, in tune to his quick-pounding heartbeat.

Patrick shrinks back a few. "Look man, I'm just sayin'. I've never seen you with a vamp chick before." He looks at me again, like he's trying to figure me out.

Julian takes a steadying breath as he stares at Patrick, his nostrils flaring. "Call me when he comes back."

Patrick nods. "Yeah, man. But don't expect me to hold him. That shit's suspicious, and some of us don't like fangs diggin' in our necks."

Julian takes another deep breath before he leaves the bar, hand still in mine as he gently tugs it. "Come on."

I keep close to him, especially now that I see the biker wolves stationed at several tables eyeing me darkly.

I should be more bothered by their menacing stares than I am, but something else is occupying my thoughts: Patrick's seen Julian with girls before? Wolves or humans? Girls he takes home for one night or gets serious about? Heated now from the jealousy consuming me, I leave Marv's with hatred in my heart... hatred toward anyone who's had the pleasure of Julian letting them in. Whether that be his heart or his pants, it doesn't matter. I can't even get in his pants... because I'm a *vampire* girl.

Not a wolf. Not a human.

A vampire.

I've never seen you with a vamp chick before...

Of course not, Patrick... because Julian doesn't want a vampire girlfriend.

Chapter 3. Biker Wolves

In the parking lot, I walk with disappointment outside Marv's, my black, four-inch Mary Janes hitting the gravel with a little more force than normal, loud *crunches* drowning out my disappointing thoughts. Julian's hand had left mine as soon as we'd passed through those doors, my safety no longer of concern now that we're outside the bar. Julian removes the pink helmet from the handlebar, handing it to me. Our ride to Marv's had been full of sexual tension (for me, anyway). Now officially done with this unrequited love business, I fully intend to keep my distance for the ride home. Rather than tightly fitting my thighs against his, I'll keep them loose. I won't wrap my arms around him and wonder what it'd feel like if he did the same to me.

What a wasted effort, all that flirting. My fears have now been confirmed: Julian doesn't go for the undead type. I put the helmet on quickly and a little roughly due to my disappointment quickly turning into anger, requiring no help adjusting the strap this time.

The bar door opens just as Julian reaches for his own helmet.

"Hey!" someone shouts, a threat in their tone as their boots crunch against the gravel past the sidewalk, nearing us. "You a vamp-fucker?"

I turn to see one of the wolf bikers standing with his beefy arms folded over his leather vest and black button-down shirt. His overgrown blonde hair hangs in front of his shadowed eyes.

Those same eyes bug out as he watches me. "The fuck you lookin' at, fangs?"

Fangs? This guy has it out for me, and I'm in no mood for it. "An ass-ugly, dick-less excuse of a wolf!" I fire back, watching his eyes bug out more prominently. "And brainless, too, coming out here to start a feud with *me*!" I bare my fangs at him, a hiss coming up my throat.

Just as I've edged toward the wolf, Julian steps in front of me, holding his hand out toward the wolf. "That's enough, now. We ain't here to start no fight."

Mr. Leather Vest looks Julian up and down from where he stands at five-seven. "You brought your dead girlfriend to a wolf bar, son. You was lookin' for a fight in doin' that."

Dead girlfriend?! There's a ringing in my ears from how pissed I've become, my vision pulsating red. I step forward, fangs out still, a growl of a sound now making its way out of me.

But Julian holds me off. "Bull shit!" Julian argues with him. "You're the one lookin' for a fight, and we ain't givin' in. Now fuck off!"

The biker wolf laughs, his head flying back with the sound. "I done seen it all, y'all!" As his head comes forward, his laughter fading, he brings two fingers to his lips and whistles through them.

Shit... he's calling his pack. I immediately back down. There's no way I can take more than one wolf. I grab Julian's forearm, his skin much hotter compared to what I'm used to from him. "Julian, we should go."

There's only two of us and God only knows how many of them. But from what I'd seen inside the bar, at least ten...

Unfortunately, before we can leave, three other wolves come out of the bar, all of them wearing the same leather vests.

"There a problem?" one of them asks Julian.

"Yeah," Julian answers. "Your friend here came lookin' to start some shit with us. We were just tryin' to leave."

"That so?" he asks, looking at the man who'd whistled, the one who started all this. "Mike, that true?"

Eyes still on Julian, Mike answers: "Naw, man. This here wolf asked me if I wanted to have a threesome with him and this corpse of his."

Julian's arm shakes under my hand, his skin burning hot, a fist forming at his side. "That ain't what happened. And she ain't no corpse!"

Now all four bikers are looking at me, causing me to shrink behind him some, one of my palms resting on his overheated cotton-tee-covered back while the other grips his trembling forearm.

"I dunno," one says, looking me up and down while licking his lips. "Dead or not, I'd do her."

Against my palm that rests on Julian's back, a vibration begins, a faint growl emerging from him.

A disgusted scowl appears on Mike's face, and he turns to look at his friend. "I know you ain't serious, bud." He points at me. "She's sixty degrees of *dead*!"

I've had enough of an awful night without adding insults to my injuries. Seeing how it's four against two (or more accurately, four against one and a half since wolves are stronger than vamps), walking away seems to be the best option. I don't want to end up as ash before I can find Denise and that serial killer. So, I release my hands from Julian's back and arm, walk to his bike, swing my leg over, straddle the cushioned seat, and hold the handlebars firmly under my hands.

"You coming?" I ask Julian.

All eyes are on me.

Julian reluctantly approaches the bike, just as laughter ensues from the bikers.

"Shoulda known she drives!" one howls with laughter.

Julian's back stiffens.

Mike pipes in: "She's got your balls in a little coin purse, ain't she?!"

More snickers and obnoxious laughs erupt.

Julian's jaw clenches. His blue-green irises brighten, on fire with rage.

I give him a warning look just before he turns and swings a punch at Mike, an excruciating crack sounding out as his fist collides with Mike's nose, sending him falling backward onto the gravel, unconscious. A growl springs from Julian's chest, deep and threatening. Undecided on how they want things to go down, two of the wolves look at each other before they simultaneously attack Julian, lunging at him with their claws out and eyes glowing just as brightly as his.

As Julian sinks one set of his claws into one of their abdomens, and the other set in the other's throat, they've inflicted their own defense wounds on him, leaving deep gashes that spew blood on Julian's neck and chest, staining his grey tee red. Still, Julian growls like a madman and shoves them off him, leaving them clutching their wounds with pained expressions as they stumble across the gravel, one of them losing his footing and falling down as he struggles to breathe from his ravaged neck.

The third wolf had abandoned his pack... or so I'd thought when I'd jumped off the bike just as he'd run off... but now I catch sight of more wolves from inside the bar coming our way. He went to get more of them to continue this fight.

I grab Julian's keys from the right jean pocket on his backside. "Get us out of here, now!"

Julian grumbles before he grabs the keys from me and hastily straddles his bike, shoving a key in the ignition and lifting the kickstand with his boot. I've hopped on behind him, helmet still on, and reflexively hold onto him for dear life as he peals out of the lot, sending bits of gravel flying toward the wolves who've just emerged from the bar.

In the street, Julian speeds well over the limit across the slick asphalt. Still dewy from the fog of an early morning, I worry we'll spin out if he doesn't watch it. His helmet still hangs from the right handlebar, but road safety isn't our biggest concern; it's the sound of roaring bikes coming after us in the distance that makes me tighten my arms around Julian and grab a fistful of the front of his shirt within my hands.

"Pull over!" I yell over the engine. "We'll hide in the woods."

"Fuck that, they'll just sniff us out."

Will they? They're going just as fast as he is, if not faster. "They're going too fast, driven by rage. By the time they pass us up, we'll take a detour and be off their radar."

With a grunt, Julian slows down and skids to a stop on the saturated earth along the side of the road. I leap off with him, and he lifts his bike and runs into the woods with me. Beyond the thick veil of brush and trunks, we watch as several motorcycles speed past where we've stopped. After the sound of their engines fade, leaving us with only the tapping of water dripping from leaves onto the soggy earth at our feet, I let out a relieved sigh. Then I tear my helmet from my head, releasing a mad abundance of dark curls and a glare from the amber of my eyes, one that's directed at the werewolf with rage issues.

"What were you thinking?!" I shout at him, angered by the fact that he'd just gotten into a fight he could have lost. "They could have ripped you apart... and me! I can only imagine what they would've done to your *vampire girlfriend* they detested so much!"

"I had it under control," he mumbles, not making eye contact with me.

Unbelievable! Hands now at my hips, eyes wide with disbelief, I move directly in front of him and stare up at him, forcing him to look at me. "Did you? Because there were ten of them and one of you... and vamps are weaker than wolves." A deep pain fills my heart. "...Did you even think about *my* safety? Or were you too busy trying to be the alpha?!"

His brows furrow with what can only be guilt. "I just lost it..."

"We can't afford for you to lose it!"

I turn away from him, running my hands through my hair, lifting the waves up from my scalp, the sticky breeze of mid-November in Texas in the strands. Julian's anger is out of control. And from what this time? Some hillbilly bikers insulting me, the *vampire chick* he could never see as anything more than the things they'd called me?

Wolves are so snobby. Just because they have a heartbeat and run hotter temperature-wise (and temperament-wise, apparently), they think they're so much better than we *sixty-degree* folk.

I scoff.

"What?" he asks, coming up behind me.

I stand there feeling defeated romantically. "I just don't get why you got so mad. You know I don't have your balls in a coin purse. Quite frankly," I say, turning around to face him once more, finding his eyes locked on mine, "I don't have any kind of hold on you. So why get so angry when they toss jabs at the corpse girl at your side? Why care enough to get cut up over it?" I sadly regard his shirt, sticking my finger through a slash on the front of it. Red is soaked in the fabric from where he'd bled there and along the collar. It's still wet from his recent wounds. I reach up and gently touch the side of his neck next, the gash that was once there now healed, the heat of his skin warm under my fingertips.

He walks away from me, leaving me standing there with fingers once warm, now colder than ever.

"It was just bull shit," he complains, leaning on his bike, his back to me. "Comin' at us to fight just 'cause I showed up with a vamp. I can show anywhere I want with anyone I damn well please."

Yearning for him turns into anger again. "Well next time you decide to pick a fight with werewolves, leave me out of it."

He glances over his shoulder, but his eyes don't meet mine. "You sayin' you don't wanna tag along anymore?"

Is that disappointment I detect? "No. I'm saying don't get into unnecessary fights anymore."

"Unnecessary," he laughs.

A hand is at my hip again. "That's funny?"

"I defended your honor and got all *cut up* like you said, and the thanks I get for it is a damn lecture."

He'd been defending my honor? Although I'm grateful to him for that, I'm also frustrated by his lack of concern for my safety. "It's just... I could've been hurt, Julian. There were so many of them."

He shakes his head, his back still facing me. "If you think I'd ever let anyone get even close to hurtin' you, you don't know me very well."

Chapter 4. Undead Hearts Break, Too

Over the fluttering in my stomach and the clenching of an undead heart, I try not to let his words affect me too deeply. Julian cares for me. I've known that for some time. He cares for me as a friend, as an ally.

But... what if he cares for me more than he lets on? He's protective of me, isn't he? He'd tucked my hand in his so the wolves at Marv's wouldn't bother me. He'd become so enraged at the bar when Patrick had made comments about Julian enjoying the sexual company of a vampire and the bite of one, too. I suppose I'd assumed he'd been mad that anyone would ever think he'd be with a vampire, as though his reputation would be tarnished if other wolves knew of his relations with one. Then again, with every insult directed at me from those wolves in the parking lot, he'd become hotter, and his voice had risen. He'd even growled.

"We should get goin'," he says, lifting his bike and beginning to take it back toward the road. "They could still sniff us out and come back."

"Well, thank you," I reply, "for defending my honor." What else can I say? More than anything, it's not words I want to respond with. I want to grab his face between my hands and kiss him. But he wouldn't kiss me back, and I'd be left feeling foolish.

"Yeah, you're welcome," he grumbles, lifting his bike over a thick branch along the ground.

On the ride back to the city, I allow myself to hold him to me as I sit behind him, knowing that after tonight, things must change. I have to savor being this close to him now, because tomorrow, I won't let myself. One thing has been made abundantly clear to me tonight: Julian and I will never be together, not the way I desire. He's protective, sure. But not because he's falling for me like I am him. He simply cares about my well-being. I must get over my infatuation with him.

At Vixen, where Julian's pulled along the curb to drop me off, I get off his bike, this time not relying on his shoulders to aid me in doing so. I remove the hot pink helmet he bought for me simply because he respects me as his partner in solving crimes, and hand it to him. He takes it and hangs it off his handlebar, just before he removes his own, his dark brown waves springing free.

"Thanks for the ride," I say from where I stand on the sidewalk next to him, the breeze that's since picked up in force swaying the flouncy hem of my deep blue dress up and around my thighs. I want to say more, but the words threatening to emerge as more of a confession for the way I feel about him are swallowed back.

In that same detached, gruff voice of his, he says, "You're welcome."

With my hands now bound behind my back, my fingers aching as they tightly entwine with each other, I refrain from placing a hand on his shoulder as I wish him goodnight. "Night, Julian."

He looks up at me, irises flickering with a light behind the blue-green. "Good night, Ivy."

I've never felt pain as great as the kind that's stirring in my chest at this moment. We vamps might not have a heart that pounds in tune to our pain, but we feel just as deeply. And this hurts. Saying goodnight to him as if I'm saying goodbye to any kind of future with him, strangles my heart.

What future can we have, anyway? He'll eventually find his mate, right? And like I've thought many times before, I'll be left in the dust of my own heart that will surely turn to ash.

I turn around, relaxing my fingers and bringing them to my front to twiddle with as I walk away from Julian.

It's then that I hear them: the motorcycles.

My spine stiffens, and I turn to look at Julian, who's sitting straighter, listening. They tracked us all the way here?

"Park in the alley!" I tell him.

He does as I've suggested, and I run alongside him toward the back of Vixen.

Once he's parked outside the back entrance, I pull my keys from the small woven crossbody bag across my front and quickly unlock the back door, gesturing for Julian to follow me. A security light is on at the front of the store, one that drifts up the hall we're taking.

Underneath Vixen is a home that used to be occupied by Farrow, a High Society member who'd used the space as a private lair of sorts. She used to lure men here to feed from them before releasing them woozy into the night. I've been permanently residing under Vixen since taking over the business, and I've redecorated extensively... and cleaned just as well. There'd been dried blood from Farrow's humans staining the floors and a mattress I've since disposed of.

That's where I lead us now: through a door I've unlocked that will take us there. I quickly lock the door behind us before I flip a switch to light up the living room beyond the wooden steps we're standing on. As we take the rickety steps one-by-one, I'm listening for engines. When I reach the end of those steps, I go straight for the office I'd set up, the lit monitors showing street views from the cameras setup outside Vixen.

Julian's followed me, and he stands behind me, watching them, too.

When the engines near, two motorcycles pass by Vixen, their riders human. No leather biker wolf vests had completed their outfits.

I slouch and sigh before relaxing against the nearest wall, eyes closed and head back against the light grey sheetrock. "That was a close one. I really thought they'd tracked us here."

"Same here."

I open my eyes to look at him, but he's still focused on the monitors.

"Don't worry," I assure him. "With the moisture in the air, our scents will fade much faster. I doubt we'll be seeing them around here."

He finally tears his eyes from the screens, his gaze falling on the living room beyond my office. He steps out onto the dark wood floor and begins to look around. I follow. He stops on the hot pink shag area rug in front of my comfy black sofa, his eyes falling on the shelves painted black that are stationed across the way from said sofa, ones filled with movies. Nestled between the shelves, the large wall-mounted television shows his reflection, a shadowed form. He walks up to my film collection, reaching out and picking up one of the slim cases.

He chuckles, "Sixteen Candles?"

"Madison gave me a copy – said it was great."

He turns the case over in his hand, reading the back. "I've seen it only once... a long time ago. You watch it yet?"

"I did."

"Whatdja think of it?"

"Sam was much too good for that Jake character." I step closer, looking at the case as well. "You know, he only became interested in her after finding that note about her wanting to have sex with him."

"Huh... never really thought about that." He sets the case back in its rightful place on the shelf, nestling it between *Fried Green Tomatoes* and *Legally Blonde*, scanning the other movie titles. "Guess I thought you'd have vampire movies, maybe horror ones. Lots of chick flicks in here..."

"I'm a bit of a romantic," I comment, observing his grin. What's he thinking? "You find my taste in films weird?"

"No. It's... cute." His grin deepens. "Really cute."

He looks around the living room again, over the small black table next to the couch housing a glittery pink lamp and a vanilla lavender candle, to the colorful abstract artwork on one wall, the three medium-sized canvases depicting the streets of Chicago (a friend I knew in the seventies commissioned them for me). In the quaint kitchen is a vintage, light pink refrigerator housing containers of blood (though he doesn't open it to find them). The cabinets are white with silver knobs. On the small pink granite counter sits a standard black microwave. I've no stove or oven, but a vampire doesn't need such things. The silver sink is empty – my usual pink mug still sitting on the counter next to the microwave, a red-stained tea bag string hanging out of it from my last cup of black tea steeped in warm blood (Madison got me hooked on bloody tea).

His gaze settles last on me. "Knew you lived here, but this is a bit different than what I imagined."

"Oh?" I ask, wondering what he could've possibly imagined. "Expected to find coffins and dripping candles littered about, did you? Perhaps an abundance of cobwebs?"

He laughs, "Sorta."

"Want to see my coffin?" I ask him, teasing ensuing.

His eyes widen a small bit. "Uh... sure."

I mosey past him, straight to my bedroom, and he follows reluctantly behind.

"In here," I purr, waiting for him to follow me in. When he does, I flip the light switch up, revealing a bed covered with a velvet black comforter printed with pink daisies and matching pillowcases adorning soft pillows.

Surprise fleets across his face, just before a grin forms. He narrows his eyes at me. "You were messin' with me."

I cross my arms in front of my chest and laugh, "Naturally."

He nods, his grin deepening, revealing a dimple in his right cheek I've often stared at.

"So, you sleep here...," he says, walking farther into the room, the tips of his fingers gliding across the comforter as he passes it by. "It's nice."

Seeing him in my bedroom, watching him touch the very comforter I snuggle against night-after-night as I sleep alone, makes me anxious with need. I'd said goodbye tonight... goodbye to romance with Julian. Yet here we are, in my bedroom, my eyes following every move he makes, my thoughts becoming fantasies of us wrapped up together in those sheets...

"Mm-hmm," I croak, silently clearing my throat.

He begins looking through the framed photos I have on a black wooden shelf, ones of me and my friends: Hailey, Madison, Dorian and Derick.

"Almost everyone's here," he comments.

I walk over to where he stands, looking at the pictures, too. "Almost?"

"I'm missin'. We should take a picture together."

He wants to be on my shelf? I smile up at him. "We can take a picture anytime." ...*Because I need a picture of you to stare at, right? Geez... a picture of me and Julian, seeing what I wish to be reflected in a photograph, one I'll stare at every single night while I yearn for him, is the last thing I need.*

"Got a camera?"

I pull my phone from my bag and hold it up. "Have this. I can print it out tonight."

Are we really doing this? Taking a picture... here? In my bedroom?

"Well, let's do it, then," he says, stuffing his hands in his front pockets.

I look at the blood stains on his skin and shirt, pointing at them. "You're covered in red."

He looks down at his shirt. "Our adventurous night can live on in the photo."

I laugh, "Adventurous night? If that's what you wish to call it...." I open the camera app and stand next to him. "Ready?" I ask, holding the camera up to face us.

"Ready," he says, his hand coming out of his pocket and settling on my right hip.

In this picture, with the way it's taken, we won't be able to capture his hand on my hip. I'd like to think he's used this picture-taking event as an excuse to touch me this way, to lean closer to me, but I know better. This pose is probably natural for him when taking pictures with someone.

I smile with him and snap the picture, looking at it after, wishing for more than just a picture with him but willing to take a special memento like this any day. "This looks good." Really, what I want to say is *we look good together*. But I can't say that.

He's looking at the picture with me, his frame hovering over mine closely, his warmth coming off him in waves against my back. "...Yeah."

What's he thinking? And why is he so close? My hands begin to shake, my stomach too.

He reaches for the phone to look at the picture closer. At least, that's what I think when he takes it from my hand. But then he sets it down on the shelf behind me and invades my space as I look up at him, the heat from his body radiating onto my skin before he's even touched me. And touch me he does, his hands finding my face and gently cupping it between his hands, his thumb skimming my chin and bottom lip, his eyes staring into mine... before he kisses me.

His lips are warm and soft against mine, and my head becomes foggy, intoxicated by him. I slip away from reality, unsure what's real anymore. Is he real? Is this kiss... real?

It can't be.

I've waited so long for my feelings to be reciprocated, and now that they are, I can't help but wonder why.

Is he finally giving into his urges, ones I've often felt he had but thought I'd imagined when he never touched me the way I'd craved? When he came so close to kissing me so many times but shut down and built walls up before he ever did? When he ignored my advances or flirtatious talk?

Why now?

Why kiss me now?

I don't want to break this kiss, to end the way his lips feel against mine, hot and demanding... the way his tongue, slick and even hotter than his lips, tangles with mine. His heart's beating louder, thudding against his ribs, pounding against my own chest as he holds me to him, his hands desperately clutching at the back of my dress.

When he lifts me and takes me over to the bed, never tearing his mouth from mine, his hands sliding up my thighs, my legs wrapping around his waist, thinking straight becomes nearly impossible.

Through the fog I'm held captive in, under the raw passion devouring us both, I still need answers. This means everything to me – his kiss, his touch... making love with him.

But I'm not his mate. This won't compare to what he'll feel with *her*, whoever she is, the girl who will strip away my happiness when she inevitably shows up to claim Julian as hers.

Behind closed lids, the cold moisture eventually breaks through and travels along my temples, into the mess of curls that is my hair. A strangled inward sob makes its way out, past my lips and onto his.

He stills, his lips pausing. He leans away to study me.

Eyes still closed, refusing to let him in on the secret that is him permanently lodged inside my heart, I only wait. ...For him to ask me why I'm crying or for him to think I'm strange and leave... I don't know.

Fingers light and gentle tickle at my cheeks, my temples.

"Ivy...," he finally breathes, his breath warm against my face. "Why are you crying?"

Because I love you.

And some day, whether after tonight (which could be a fleeting one-time thing for him when I crave forever), or many years into the future when *she* shows up... eventually, he'll leave.

And all I'll have is this hole inside my heart – a bleeding, open wound that will never fully heal.

"I can't," I cry, a whisper of words releasing my pain.

"Can't what?" he whispers back.

"Can't keep hurting myself."

"Hurting yourself?"

Ah, confessions of the heart... always a tragic thing to behold... and awkward for him, once the truth seeps out of me.

"Loving you," I finally say, my lower lip trembling. "Loving you the way you'll love your mate, the way you can never love me."

He presses his forehead to mine, releasing a deep breath through his nose, tickling the skin of mine. "Oh, Ivy..."

"I know," I whisper still. "I know how ridiculous—"

"No," he says, his nose gently rubbing against mine, his mouth grazing my quivering lips. "You *are* my mate."

"What?" I ask, finally opening my eyes to see his now closed lids, his long dark brown lashes matching the curls falling over his brow.

His brows pull in. "I knew it the moment I saw you."

"I... I don't understand."

He shakes his head, his lips still just hairs from mine, his breath hot against them. "I couldn't claim you. For so long, I denied you, denied our bond... because I couldn't afford the distraction."

This can't be right. It's too good to be true, me being... his.

And it's too painful, him rejecting me this entire time...

"I just... can't anymore. I can't deny you," he continues, his lips touching mine, the gentlest of contact, as he works his mouth against mine, beckoning me to kiss him back.

He's been *denying* me, causing me the most horrific pain in doing so, all because he'd seen me as a distraction. And now, after what? Suffering long enough as well... he's claiming me?

Once I've stiffened under his touch, fighting to be released from whatever magical bond that's taking us under, he stops. He pulls away, but he doesn't go far. No, his weight is still atop me. My legs are still firmly planted against his hips, my body and heart demanding what my mind wishes to now deny.

"Ivy?" he asks, his voice on guard.

"You made me feel insane," I say, looking into his eyes, searching for something... but I don't know what. Perhaps something to ease the pain

I still feel? Something to change this all so it stops hurting altogether? "You denied me. All those times I yearned for you, burned for you, ached in the most excruciating of ways, you... *knew*. All along, you knew I was yours... and you... denied me."

He hadn't claimed me. He'd pushed me away. He'd rejected me as his mate.

"I was afraid," he admits, looking at me with sadness in the depths of his shadowed, grey eyes.

"So was I," I whisper, my voice quivering, "...of a love that consumed me from the inside out, a love that burned beneath the surface... unrequited."

His brows pull in deeper. "It's not unrequited. I do love you."

I've waited to hear those words from him for so long, but now everything is tainted by me knowing the truth. While I'd been suffering and yearning for him, believing us too different or him indifferent, he wanted me too? He'd... denied me.

"No," I say, clenching my jaw tight before releasing it, afraid now of my own words. "You rejected me, denied me... left me to burn away painfully."

His voice is low, scorned: "You don't think I burned? You don't think I yearned and ached and hated myself for denyin' you? You don't think I laid awake at night tossin' and turnin', ready and willin' to come for you, to make you mine? I did. I wanted it so bad... wanted *you* so bad." His eyes travel away from my eyes, focusing on my lips. "I'll always want you."

"That's too bad," I seethe, new tears emerging, blurring his image. It's better if I don't see him anyway, so I can't see the pain I'm about to inflict on him. "I now... deny *you*."

A gasp escapes him, a strangled sound as my words slice into him. "No, Ivy... please."

I squeeze my eyes shut, feeling cool tears quickly sliding along my temples, travelling the same path as the others... tears he'd caused. Pain he'd caused. I inhale deeply, unsteadily, as grief wrecks me anew. "Get out."

Chapter 5. Bye, Bye Wolfies

It's been almost twenty-four hours since I kicked Julian out of my bed.

His reaction had hurt me even more than I already was, creating a hole that gaped much bigger than the last. His jaw had been open with shock, his eyes wide with pain, their depths haunted. But he'd done as I'd asked. He'd left, and the last I'd heard of him had been the roar of his motorcycle's engine speeding away from Vixen.

Now, at nearly midnight, the arrival of another day having met me, I'm standing behind the register at Vixen, staring off into space thinking about the decision I'd made to tell him to leave. I question whether I'd been too harsh or not, or if my response to discovering he'd been denying me this entire time as his mate was justified. Should I have been so hurt? Wasn't he just trying to stay focused so we could stick to our mutual goals: find the serial killer vampire, find Denise?

I glare at nothing in particular. Distraction or not, he'd denied me. I'd *suffered*.

I suppose I want him to feel the same pain I've been subjected to these last few months. I'd never felt so attached to someone, so completely overtaken with lust and an undeniable need to have them. I'd *craved* him... and I still do. It's unfortunate, really, being the mate of a wolf who has so many unresolved issues, their focus so absorbed by revenge that they deny the one magical thing gifted to them in life.

It's that same magic that'd turned Madison – changing her from a vampire to a wolf.

Julian will never change me. He'd be binding himself to me in doing so, and let's face it... he's more content with the way things are to allow such a *distraction* to ruin his chances of finding Denise.

As for me? I've been a vampire for decades. I'm comfortable. When I was human, things were hardly simple, and getting the things my family required to survive was sometimes impossible... like nourishment, medicine, jobs. As a vamp, I can feed when I want, picking from the many willing customers at Club Vudu or the men who pursue me in hopes of having sex. I don't suffer from illnesses, so medication will never be needed, therefore I can't be denied it. Before Vixen, I was paid by the High Society to keep the streets clean and to assist with several tasks at both Vudu and Vixen, like bookkeeping. I lived in a lavish apartment, supplied with all the blood bags a girl could dream of having. Now, I'm supplied with sustenance from willing parties and sleeping in a quaint little home beneath my shop. Vixen is mine now. I'm perfectly content with the way things are.

Except... I'm not.

My shoulders slump as I stop lying to myself.

Truth is, I'm not sure how I'd fare as a wolf. They're certainly more powerful than vampires, stronger and faster... and they don't require blood to survive. They have hot blood rushing through their veins from a heart that beats, making them warmer and much closer to feeling human than we vamps.

Maybe that's what I'm afraid of... feeling more human like I was before, when life was less kind to me and my loved ones.

It's probably for the best, Julian and I taking some time apart. He needs to figure out what he *wants*, not what he can no longer *deny*. I don't want to be the woman he chases after because of some magical force he's having a hell of a time evading. I want to be the woman he wants and needs... and loves.

With a heart that sinks even deeper in realizing that will never be, knowing he's too fixated on other more pressing matters, I move myself away from the register and begin stocking to take my mind off things. Perhaps the angst I feel within my chest will soon dissipate when my hands are busy.

At a quarter till one, a new dread settles over me when two men walk into Vixen. Before I've even turned to face them, I know what they are: wolves. My spine has tingled and stiffened in response to their arrival, a natural response we vamps have when other supernatural beings enter our space. Given my altercation with vampire-hating wolves last night, their presence can't be good.

I turn, fuzzy hot pink handcuffs in hand, recognizing them as the two wolves who'd attacked Julian at Marv's after he'd knocked their friend named Mike out. They're wearing the same black leather vests they had on last night.

They've tracked me here.

My throat closes up just as my entire frame has stiffened. I force the lump in my throat down. I can't show my fear.

"Can I help you with something?" I ask, hoping my cold tone will indicate that they're beginning a war they most certainly don't want.

They look around the shop, slowly making their way through it, refusing to acknowledge me. One of them grabs a chemise off a rack – a black lacy piece – before he settles his glowing gaze upon me. Eyes yellow like the sun, I see his darkness visibly. Yellow eyes are a sure sign that a wolf (or a vamp, for that matter) has gone completely dark... evil.

"You ever wear somethin' like this?" he asks, looking over my figure. He's the one from last night who said he'd "*do*" me. He's roughly five-eleven, with a thick frame and disheveled brown hair.

I refuse to answer him.

He sets the chemise down, his focus moving to the dildos on the wall next to him. "You ever played with one of these?" He looks at me again, waiting for a reaction from me.

I keep my face blank, my mouth closed.

The other wolf, the thinner one with lighter hair and a curious grin, has made his way over to the register. "Bet you make lots of money sellin' this kinda shit."

I glance at him now. Are they just here to rob me... or do something much more sinister?

The other wolf who'd questioned my taste in lingerie moves closer in my direction. "You sellin' more than what we see out here?"

I shake my head.

He grins, looking me over again, biting his lower lip. "Maybe you just give it up free to a wolf. Hmm, vampire? You like wrappin' your legs around a stronger being, feelin' our power inside you?"

I know what he's insinuating: that I have sex with wolves for kicks. Little does he know, I've never been with one, not even the one I want... the *only* one I want.

"I mean, we seen you with that wolf last night," he continues, confirming my suspicions, glancing at his partner, who's still by the register. "We know you like our kind. Maybe it even excites you, gettin' somethin' a little extra than what your dead kind can give you."

I jump when the register is smashed to bits, the other wolf having busted it with a solid fist. Taking cash from it, he stuffs the bills in his pockets.

The thicker wolf, the one coming closer to me, eyes the wall of toys to his left. "Maybe you like it when someone uses this here stuff on you... huh?" He turns and sends his right fist through the wall, breaking the sheetrock and sending packaged goods on the floor.

I've jumped back, straight into a wall behind me.

He begins to grab packages off racks still holding a few, tossing them everywhere, tearing the metal racks off the walls as he does and sending them flying as well with bits of more sheetrock.

His friend begins to do the same, busting through the glass shelves holding lubricants and condoms, the glass loudly shattering under his fists. He kicks over another glass stand, sending it and the contents crashing to the pink carpeted floor in pieces. He spots books on a shelf and grabs them, ripping the pages out and tossing them in the air.

The two of them are laughing as they destroy everything in sight.

And it's time for me to run... before I lose my chance. I dart for the hall leading to the back door, but when I reach the end of the hall, and I'm pushing on the door to open it, I realize with horror that something's blocking it on the other side. The larger wolf has caught up to me, his figure blocking the light from the other end of the hall, his illuminated yellowed eyes darkly watching me.

"You've had your fun," I shout at him. "Now get out!"

"This here ain't the fun we came for."

Oh, no... they came for me... to have *fun* with me. Their idea of fun could be anything from torture and torment, to rape and murder. Perhaps both.

"I got the cash and some other shit," the other wolf hollers from behind this one. "Let's go!"

"Naw," his friend says, his eyes glowing even brighter, his voice lowering threateningly: "I want somethin' else before we leave."

My gut is aching in warning, as is my un-beating heart. The cool blood trickling through my veins is now fueled by adrenaline, my limbs quivering in response. Using all my strength, I back into the door, pushing it, willing whatever is blocking it to bust. What sounds like metal groaning from being bent sounds out, and the door begins to move. Of course, there isn't enough space for me to escape through, and I've run out of time. The wolf has come for me, his large black biker boots having stomped across the small hall, his beefy hands grabbing my shoulders and pulling me forward, hauling me across the space of the hall, sending me stumbling back into the shop and falling onto the thin pink carpet, the fibers burning my palms and knees as I land.

His friend appears stunned, fearful even, as he looks down at me. "You said we were just gonna scare her." He appears confused as he watches his wolf friend stalk toward me.

I quickly get my wits about me and scramble to my feet, running from them. But the wolf who'd tossed me onto the floor is so much faster than me. He's reached me just as I've reached the front door of the shop. I'm grabbed by the back of my grey dress and pulled against the overly heated front of him, his large hand coming over my mouth as I begin to scream. I bite his hand, and just as he's growled and released his hold over my mouth, I scream for Julian, my throat quickly becoming raw from how forceful the sound is.

Whether our bond has been completed or not, I hope he can still feel me, that my fear somehow calls out to him just as clearly as his name ripping from my throat.

The hand is back, as is an arm that's snaked its way around my waist, pulling me back into a burning chest.

Still not willing to participate in this plan, the other wolf has stood by, scratching the top of his head anxiously. "Come on, Jeb! If her wolf finds out, he'll tear us apart."

"He ain't gonna find out," Jeb argues, a certain excitement in his tone as he continues to drag me back, my flats coming right off my feet as I've kicked my legs. "We ain't leavin' nothin' for him to find."

With that, a sharp pain begins at my shoulder and radiates down my arm and across my chest, ripping another scream from me, one that's muffled against his palm.

"How's it feel gettin' bit, *fangs*?!" he howls, laughing.

Dizzy from his bite, the pain spreading through the entirety of my upper half, I can barely focus through the blurred and shifting images in front of me.

A laugh rises from his friend. "Fuck, dude! You bit her! She taste dead or what?"

Jeb laughs as he fiddles with the strap of my dress under where he'd bitten me, before he pulls it down, the strap snapping, the upper half of my dress coming down forcefully as he yanks at it. "Tastes thick, sweet... wonder what she'll feel like."

"I want some," his friend says, now coming forward, his footing hesitant.

I can't bear another bite, even if the one at my shoulder has begun to heal, clearing my vision well enough to see the other wolf's face coming close to mine. He leans down, his lips teasing at my other shoulder as I struggle against the wolf holding me captive against him.

Just as his canines graze my skin, the wolf readying himself to tear into me, he's pulled back with a gurgled grunt. His eyes roll back, and his mouth is left hanging open in shock. Standing next to him, is Julian. The wolf is tossed on the floor, his heart in Julian's hand from where it'd been ripped out of his back.

Eyes glowing fiercely, a snarl on his lips and blood dripping from his hand, he regards Jeb with a growl. "Release her."

"You fuckin' killed Tommy!" Jeb shouts, removing his hand from my mouth. His claws are at the back of my neck now, pulling my head back, sharp tips digging in.

A pained scream makes its way out of me, just as tears swim in my eyes as I stare at the spinning white ceiling tiles.

"Take another step and I'll take her head off!" Jeb warns.

Another growl emerges from Julian. "Hurt her and I'll rip your fuckin' throat out!"

Jeb's claws loosen against my neck, his next move unsure as he silently shifts his feet. When he begins to pull me back, toward the hall, I hear Julian following, his boots hitting the carpet in determination.

He stops when Jeb yells: "One more fuckin' step, and she's ash!"

The wolf's hold on my neck has loosened enough now for me to see Julian. There's both anger and desperation on his face – his jaw is clenched, and thick brows are pulled down harshly above his vibrantly lit eyes.

Jeb chuckles low, a whisper of a sound, as he breathlessly pulls me closer to the back exit. Once there, he pushes against it, the metal groaning as it'd done when I'd pushed on the door.

In that moment, he becomes distracted, his focus now on getting the door open, his claws removed from my neck entirely. Only one of his hands clutches one of my wrists behind my back. I quickly pull us forward, twisting to the side to haul him toward Julian. His claws rip open the inside of my wrist with a searing pain as he lets go of me, stumbling toward Julian.

Julian steps forward, grabbing Jeb by his neck, his claws digging into the wolf's flesh, coating his hand crimson. His other hand reaches into Jeb's chest, knocking him back with a powerful force, just before he's pulled forward, his heart ripped right out of him. Jeb's body slouches before Julian drops him to the floor, tossing his bleeding heart on top of him with a disgusting wet sound as it hits his back.

On my knees now, grasping my bleeding wrist against the fabric of my dress, I stare at Julian, relieved he'd come for me.

"You knew?" I ask him, watching him come to me and kneel down to look at my wrist.

Injuries from wolves are slower to heal than ordinary ones. This one still bleeds, but it's slowly closing up. Julian cleans his bloodied hands as best as he can against the thighs of his jeans, but red still stains them. He rips the left sleeve of his navy cotton tee off and makes a bandage from the fabric, securing it around my wrist, his fingers so warm and caring against my ravaged skin. I stare at his exposed bicep from where he'd ripped the sleeve of his shirt off, admiring the way his muscles bulge as he tightens the makeshift bandage.

"Felt you," he admits, finishing tying the bandage. "...Heard you."

Had he been near when I'd screamed? "Heard me? You were close?"

"No... I was on my way back to Whispering Creek. Had a lead on Denise. ...I felt your fear before you screamed my name, but I heard your scream in the back of my mind, almost like a whisper. Should've kept close by, but..." He shakes his head, frustration evident in his downward brows.

"But?"

He huffs, "Wanted to give you space. Dumbest damn thing I've ever done."

I can't help but smile. I'd wanted space, but since having made werewolf enemies, it'd been unwise on my part to want that distance. Not to mention, I've felt so completely torn apart since denying him last night. Having him here with me now feels right, comforting, peaceful. "I know what you mean."

Julian laughs, a small sound, as he examines my healing shoulder and the ripped strap of my grey dress. It's completely ruined, this dress, all ripped and bloodied now... and it was one of my favorites, too.

One of my favorites...

Stupid wolves...

His face blurs, his features shifting and blending together as I lean toward him, a lightheadedness overcoming me. Now that the adrenaline has left my system, my body has grown weaker from the wounds I'd endured.

"You're still bleedin' here," he observes, his warm fingers delicately touching my shoulder.

"Mm, he bit me," I confirm, that wooziness taking me further under as I lean forward still.

"Ivy...," Julian worriedly says, holding me steady by the tops of my arms. "You don't look so good."

I mumble my next words: "Lost too much blood... and the bite... wounds like that take a lot out of us."

"Do you... Do you need to feed?"

"Mm..."

"Where's your—"

I slump heavier now, his voice seeming farther off than before. I can still feel his presence, his heated palms holding me up.

"Ivy..."

Now an echo, that delectably deep voice and syrupy smooth southern accent of his calls to me from every corner of my mind. "Mm?"

I register that he's pulled me closer, that I'm sitting more in his lap than on the carpet of my shop. Warmth is beneath my lips, a throbbing heat making my gums and the space between my thighs throb away...

"Bite me," Julian urges.

Chapter 6. Claimed

Bite me...

Words so sweet, so inviting, so... undeniable.

Across his heated flesh, at the most sensitive part of the inside of his neck, I trace my tongue across his skin, his quickened beating heart as it pumps blood through the very vein I ache to pierce, moving under my cool tongue. I caress his skin with the ends of my teeth, preparing him for my bite. Finally applying pressure, harder, deeper, I sink my fangs into him, his warmth filling my mouth – the hot, thick, coppery taste just as intoxicating as the kiss we'd shared last night.

His breath hitches as he feels his own mounting desire taking him under with me. His arms hold me tighter, his hips twitch beneath mine. Gently sucking, I slowly take his blood as my own. The dull ache inside my heart and the throbbing between my thighs demands more from him. I reach between us, pulling at the button of his jeans, sliding the zipper away and reaching inside, feeling how much he wants me, too. Gently, I pull him free and settle myself over him while I feed, ripping the barrier of underwear between us, drawing him inside me, the two of us moaning as I do.

One of his hands is at my back, the other grabbing hold of the bare skin of my hip, his palm cupping my bottom, his fingers digging into my flesh. He pushes his hips against mine as I ride him.

"You're mine," he growls low, deep, before he trails hungry kisses along my shoulder where I'd been bitten.

I quicken my movements, the hard length of him sliding between my folds so perfectly, filling me entirely.

I pull my fangs from his neck, gliding my tongue across his skin to heal my marks faster. I hold onto his shoulders, holding him closer to me, as I move faster and rougher against him. He pulls the thin red lace of my bra down, his tongue slowly licking at one of my nipples before he takes it into his mouth, gently sucking on me as he rubs his tongue against the bud. My head falls back as helpless moans escape me.

He nips at my chin, soon taking hold of my lips as I tilt my face to his, his tongue diving deep into my mouth, tasting himself. He moans against my lips, his kiss becoming harder, more demanding, as he molds his mouth to mine. I bite at his lower lip, drawing blood and sucking it before it heals, making him moan again. His hips are urgent against mine, as he lifts them in tune with my movements.

As a pleasureful pressure grows inside me, I practically shatter against him, clutching him to me and moaning inside his mouth while my hips slow with each ripple of my release. Julian growls out, finding his, too.

Breathless unlike me, he still grips my hips beneath his hands, his thick fingers hot against my bare skin. In my mind, whispers sound out, my own voice mingling with his as whispers of my name flutter about in his voice, tangling with the promise of forever.

You're mine, he'd said.

He'd bound himself to me. And I'd accepted, gladly riding him, drinking him, claiming him right back.

I let out a satisfied sigh. After decades of waiting, unaware that I was waiting for him, I'm finally sated... content. I thought I knew contentment, that my undead life was precisely the thing I needed. But then Julian had crashed into me unexpectedly, and now that we've bound ourselves to each other, any fears and uncertainties I'd had about becoming a wolf melt away. With him is exactly where I'm meant to be.

But does he feel the same? He'd claimed me in a moment of passion, any rational thoughts he may have had buried deep, just as deeply as he'd buried himself inside me. Regardless of any regrets he may soon have, what's done is done. We're mated.

Still wrapped-up with him, legs spread and hips straddling his, I look over at the wolves he'd killed, their bloodied, ripped-out hearts and bodies staining my brand-new, beautiful pink carpet.

Unsure now of what he'll do or say, I begin to slide off his lap, a small moan coming from him as I do.

Seeming content, a grin on his stubbled face, he keeps his gaze locked with mine. "That was…"

"Mind-blowing?" I guess. That's how it'd felt for me, anyway.

He sighs, an almost surprised sound. "Yeah…"

Is he surprised? "Didn't expect that?"

"No… not exactly."

My heart sinks. "What did you expect?" Had I been compared to the countless others, the wolves he's likely slept with?

Brows now higher, mouth partially open, he thinks of his answer for a few moments before responding: "I knew it'd be amazing, but…" He watches me, his gaze darkening while I adjust my bra, pulling the lace back up to conceal my breasts.

"But?" I ask, glancing at his member still on display.

A flicker of light begins to show more brightly behind his irises. "Ivy…"

I wait for him to say more, but he simply shakes his head, tearing his eyes from mine, before he puts his penis away and zips his pants. He stands and looks at the dead wolves on the floor. "We should clean this up." He holds his hand out, waiting for me to take it from where I still sit on my knees on the floor.

Still feeling his release inside me, a wetness beginning to coat my thighs, disposing of dead wolves is hardly the thing I desire at the moment. "Allow me to clean myself up first?"

"Of course."

I take his offering hand and allow him to pull me up, vaguely wondering as he does, if he's ever not used condoms with the other women he's been with? Being a vamp, the ability to reproduce is impossible. I'm sure he took that into account.

"I'll need to call Marv," Julian says, brushing a hand through the curls on top his head. "Tell him what happened."

Marv... as in the werewolf bar Marv's? "Marv... the bar owner?"

"Yeah, he'll need to know... give the news to the pack."

"Why? So they can gather in a mob and come after us? Shouldn't we just get rid of the evidence and move on?"

He regards their corpses with a crowded brow and a low growl in his chest. "No. They came for my mate. Their pack should know they'll end up the same as these two assholes if they try it again."

If I had a heartbeat like him, it'd have fluttered excitedly in that moment, hearing him confirm that I'm his mate. Will there be no regrets on his end, then, for binding himself to me?

He looks at me next, his eyes travelling over my face, studying me. "Somethin' wrong?"

I shrug, a small smile forming upon my lips. "I just like the way that sounds, you calling me your mate."

He smiles, too.

"Anyway," I say, pulling up the ripped strap of my dress briefly. "I should bathe and change." I turn around to enter the door nearby, the one leading to my home beneath the shop, when Julian says my name, causing me to stop.

"I shouldn't have left. I just... I thought space wasn't such a bad thing." Guilt is now in his voice: "I said I'd never let anyone hurt you, but... I failed you."

I turn around now, finding his saddened eyes on me. "You didn't fail me."

His brows knit even closer together. "I did. I wasn't here."

I don't like this guilt that's weighing him down. I can feel it inside me, pulling at my heart. I can't allow him to torment himself over something that wasn't his fault. "Are we supposed to remain attached at the hip? We can't be together twenty-four-seven, you know. You were chasing a lead, something that's important to you... finding Denise."

He shakes his head, determination in his voice: "Not more important than you."

This is news to me. Hasn't his sole mission in life been to find that traitorous woman? He'd been on his way to her... "You felt my fear and turned around, even though you were so close..."

He walks toward me, each step careful, decided, before he stands in front of me, his warmth radiating into me. "I'll always choose you."

I offer a small smile, my shoulders lifting slightly. "Now that we've made it official?"

He takes one of my hands in his, mine seeming even smaller as it rests in the tan, bloodied, calloused cocoon of his. His eyes are burning into mine as they often do. His voice is softer now: "Even before that. Why do you think I recruited you to help me find Denise? I needed excuses to be around you, to be close... even if I didn't intend to claim you right away. I shouldn't have waited as long as I did, and I'm sorry for that. Truly, I am. I thought I was doin' the right thing, that I couldn't be both sides of the wolf: the mated one and the vengeful one. I wanted to be fair to you and not drag you down with all my burdens."

I touch the side of his face with my free hand, the soft pieces of an emerging beard tickling the tips of my fingers. "You're not burdensome, Julian. I want to find Denise just as much as you do."

He places one of his hands over mine, holding it in place against his cheek, his eyes closing as he leans into my palm. "That's the thing... I was selfish before, havin' you come with me to chase after the darkest of beasts."

Does he not want me involved any longer? "What are you saying?"

He opens his eyes, settling them on mine again. "I'm sayin' I'm more afraid of losin' you than never findin' those who've wronged us."

He's choosing me over revenge? "You're... giving up the hunt?"

He nods.

As much as I've wished for him to want me, to let himself love and be loved, I refuse to let him give up so easily on something so important to him. "I can't let you do that."

"'Course you can."

"No, Julian, we're—"

"Mates," he interrupts. "You come first."

I rub his stubble under my thumb. "We're also a *team*. She's the reason you were tortured, the reason you were hurt so profoundly."

I want to cry remembering that room I'd seen at the High Society's mansion not that long ago. Julian had been strapped to a metal table and tortured with aconite and tools for several hours... all because Denise had turned him and his pack in so she could be pardoned for her part in them helping Madison and Dorian deal with the Society. He'd helplessly watched them be slaughtered before he'd been dragged off to be relentlessly tortured.

As angry as I am at Denise, I'm just as angry with myself, because if I'd ended the High Society much sooner, rather than carefully calculating every move I made, waiting for the perfect moment to begin picking them off, Julian never would have lost his pack. He never would've been tortured.

"Your heart is weighed down with guilt," he says, rubbing my hand, warming my skin.

"I feel responsible as well," I admit, "because I was once part of the High Society. I kept plotting their end instead of acting to make it happen. Had I acted sooner, all of this could have been avoided."

"You're not responsible for what Denise did. She broke our code and turned us in. *She* betrayed us... not you."

I want to accept what he's said, to ease the heaviness in my heart, but it's difficult for me to do that. Part of me wants peace with Julian, but another part craves revenge just as desperately as he does. Ending Denise means ending this pain. For both of us.

Still staring into the eyes of the wolf who's become mine, I want justice for him. I want Denise to suffer for leading her pack to their own executions, and for Julian's suffering.

I unclench my teeth and take a deep breath. "We have to make her pay."

Chapter 7. All Things Tragic

It's a tad quieter in Marv's at four in the afternoon on a Wednesday. The music is low compared to the last time I was here, a classic rock song playing. Only one customer is in here: a lone wolf sipping a beer in one of the booths.

"Holy shit," Patrick exclaims when he sees me walk into Marv's with Julian at my side. I'm wearing a sleeveless dark red sundress that ends mid-thigh and little black flats, my exposed porcelain skin brightened from the many open windows sending sunlight throughout the establishment. "A vamp walkin' around in broad daylight?! I've seen it all now!"

Julian grunts before he leans on the bar counter in front of where Patrick stands. "Vamps don't burn in the sun, dipshit."

Patrick's brows immediately pull down, a scowl forming. "Screw you, Napper."

Julian simply laughs. "Yeah, yeah, I'm an asshole. Where's Marv?"

Patrick folds his arms across his chest as he looks between us. "Office. ...Why?"

"Got some bad news for him," Julian answers solemnly.

"Yeah?"

"Yeah. Two wolves from that damn biker pack came for my mate last night. Had to put 'em down."

My stomach still trembles with joy every time he calls me that.

Patrick seems surprised, his brows lifting once more. "No shit? You mated? To who?"

Julian lets out an exasperated sigh, rubbing the stubble along his jaw as he looks at Patrick incredulously. "You really are short a few fries, ain't ya?" He nods toward me. "She's standin' right here."

Patrick looks at me, then Julian, then me again. An amused smile forms, and a small chuckle comes out of him. "Shut the fuck up. Since when do wolves have vamps for mates?"

So it *is* uncommon, then... and Patrick is clearly against relations between the two species.

Julian leans on the counter, his chin resting against his palm as he eyes Patrick as though he's grown bored. "Since now. Marv got time for visitors or what?"

Patrick's eyes slowly leave mine, his curiosity still sparked. "...Yeah... uh, yeah his door's always open."

Julian removes his hand from under his chin before he grabs my hand, leading me toward a set of double doors. "All right, then."

"I got questions still," Patrick calls.

Good luck getting answers...

Even I don't know how this works, how a vamp and a wolf can become mates, the apparently dominating species taking over the vamp's body once they're bitten by their mate, changing them from a vamp to a wolf...

When will Julian change me? ...*Will* he change me?

Julian knocks on a door with a scuffed-up black sticker in the center of it that reads *Office* in bold, white letters.

"Come on in," a voice shouts, one I can only assume belongs to Marv.

Julian turns the worn brass knob, walking in slowly, looking around the space. The walls are unpainted wood panels like the rest of the restaurant. Above the chipped-up desk Marv sits at, his back to us, hangs three busts of animals, their heads stuffed and mounted on decorative wooden pieces: two deer and a moose between them. Paperwork is scattered on the desk, and Marv is flipping between pages. He's an older wolf, a black and grey braid travelling down to the center of his back.

"Came bearing bad news," Julian says, getting straight to the point.

Marv remains focused on his papers, muttering: "Yeah?"

He must be used to bad news.

"Two of the wolves from a biker pack came after my mate last night... customers of yours. They're dead."

Marv's back stiffens, his focus now away from the paperwork. He slowly turns around in the squeaky swivel chair to face us. He appears fifty with a beard much greyer than his hair, wearing an unbuttoned Henley, the thick hairs on his chest showing. His jean jacket looks as though it's been rubbed in dirt, the jeans on his legs clinging to his stout thighs just as dirty. His curious blue eyes look me over for a moment before he gives Julian his undivided attention. "Why'd they do that?"

Julian shrugs. "'Cause she's a vamp. They saw me with her the night before last and came outside to start shit with us about us bein' together."

Is that sadness I detect in Marv's expression? He rubs his long, greying beard. "I assume Mike led them out?"

Mike must start brawls often... or perhaps he expresses his hatred for vampires all the time.

"Outside the bar, yeah... but he wasn't there last night."

Marv sighs now, shaking his head. "That boy ain't right... always lookin' for trouble. I'll call up Luis, break the news to him. It's his pack. That shit ain't gonna stand with him." He mutters now: "Mike might get booted for startin' the whole damn thing. Serves him right..."

Not every wolf I've encountered has had issues with the undead. For every wolf that hates us, there's another that doesn't. Marv clearly falls in the group of those who don't have a problem with my kind. But given how many in Luis' pack had started a fight with Julian and I, I can't help but suspect that they're all fang-haters. I doubt Mike will be booted.

"Anyway," Julian says, shuffling his feet, "if they want their bodies, we've got 'em stored in a big freezer."

At the mansion, where the High Society used to store humans they'd drained until they could make arrangements to dispose of them, is a large walk-in freezer. Since moving into the mansion, Madison and Dorian were using it to store meat... before we needed it for bodies, anyway, having shown up at their doorstep verrrrrrry early this morning with hopeful smiles and two dead werewolves in the back of Julian's old truck (he doesn't always drive that motorcycle, you know).

Marv's eyes had drifted to the wooden floorboards in thought, but as Julian's spoken, he looks up once more. "I'll ask. Say, you find Denise last night?"

"Kinda got busy..."

Marv's brows furrow, and he clenches one of his fists against his thigh. "Damn."

Marv wants her caught, too. "She might still be around," I say. "Might still be right here in Whispering Creek." Julian and I didn't just come out here to talk to Marv.

Marv begins to chew at his thumbnail. "Yeah, maybe... two-timin' bitch."

He definitely wants her caught.

"Anyway," he sighs, standing up at about five-six. "Thanks for stoppin' by. Let me know if you catch her."

"Will do," Julian says. "Thanks for givin' me the tip about her whereabouts."

So Marv had been the one to tell Julian where Denise was last night...

"Any time. If I know somethin', you'll be the first to know. Those of us who value loyalty don't take too kindly to betrayal. You'll find plenty of wolves who will back you up on lookin' for her. Hell, she might not make it out of Whisperin' Creek. News travels fast 'round here. She might already be six feet under."

A low growl sounds out deep in Julian's chest. "Let's hope not. As the former leader of the pack she betrayed, I'd like to deal with her myself."

Marv's lips form a tight line. "Yeah... I don't blame you on that one." Hope fills his eyes suddenly. "...You by chance lookin' to start a new pack?"

"Not sure. Startin' one up takes a lot of work and devotion. I've got my hands full at the moment." He eyes Marv curiously. "Why do you ask?"

I'd like to know the answer to that as well. Does Marv know wolves looking for one?

Marv shrugs. "Oh, I was just thinkin' it'd be a shame for you not to lead a new pack, that's all. You're one of the good ones, ya know?"

I lean into Julian. I hadn't had the pleasure of seeing him lead a pack before, but he has all the right qualities. When we'd gone after Catherine, the ringleader of the High Society, he'd begun leading the way at a certain point, his natural instincts taking over. Authoritative and confident, we'd all trusted him, following his lead... right to Catherine.

"Thanks," Julian says, shaking Marv's hand. "I'll let you know if things change."

"Most def, we'll see ya around." He directs his attention to me. "Good to meet you... uh?"

"Ivy," I answer, shaking his hand as well.

"Ivy, all right." The shake lasts a couple seconds before he releases me. "Well y'all don't get into too much trouble, yeah?"

"We'll try our best," Julian morbidly laughs, leading us out of Marv's office.

We pass by the bar, but Patrick's busy serving a couple human customers, therefore losing the opportunity to question us like he'd intended to. His disappointed gaze follows us out.

"Well that was fun," I comment, grabbing my pink helmet from the handlebar of Julian's bike. "Where to next? Do we know where in Whispering Creek Denise is?"

He grabs the strap under my chin and fastens it. "Crisp. It's a little health food shop about fifteen out. Marv thinks she's workin' there. One of his wolves spotted her."

One of his wolves... "He has a pack?"

"Yeah, he and his wife run it. They've taken in a few loners over the years and built it up. Got 'em jobs and all. Marv's a good guy. I've known him for over ten years now."

And how long has he been a wolf for? I never have asked... I get on the bike after he's settled himself up front, my arms snaking their way around his torso, appreciating the way his muscles flex under my fingers. Instead of stiffening like I've grown used to, he remains relaxed now that he no longer resists me.

"When were you turned?"

He revs the engine and takes off. "Early sixties. You?"

"Thirties," I answer, quickly turning the tables back around on him. "So, what's your story? Did you choose to be a wolf, or was this something that just... happened?" ...Like in my case.

"Chose it. Was a runaway. Man took me in, introduced me to his family... his pack. I found out what they were, and when I was twenty-two, asked to be turned."

If Julian already had a pack, why did he start a new one? "So, you were part of a pack before you started your own. What happened with the other pack?"

"I left it. We disagreed on some things."

"Like?"

"Like sharin' wives."

Sitting behind him, he can't see my bulging eyes. "What?!"

"They were a polygamous community."

"A polyg— and you lived there?!"

He shrugs under the worn material of his jean jacket. "Yeah, for six years. I was sixteen when I was taken in. ...Shared around quite a bit up until two years before I left."

Shared around?! "I'm sorry, what?!"

He grunts, clearing his throat. "Yeah... the uh... well, the females liked havin' me."

"And how old were these women?"

"Older, twenties and thirties."

I can't help but clench my arms around him tighter. "And they slept with you?! When you were sixteen?!"

"Like I said, it was a polygamous community. The husbands and wives all shared each other. None of 'em were mated like we are; none were committed like us."

He thinks I'm upset about the sharing of spouses? "I'm more concerned that they took you in and molested you."

He stiffens, his back straightening. "Part of why I left, Ivy. At sixteen, I thought it was weird and all, but I was *sixteen*. I had shelter, food... people sayin' we were family when I never really had one. I didn't wanna let it all go and lose what I thought were missin' pieces finally comin' together. ...But when they wanted me to take a wife a couple years after turnin', I just couldn't do it. So, I left. Cut to ten years later, I had my own pack, a new family. And it wasn't no polygamous pack, neither."

Julian was a runaway, alone in the world until he met a pack of polygamous wolves. They'd taken advantage of him, but I'm glad he'd finally left their clutches. "Glad to hear it... about the new pack, I mean. Not so much the missing pieces... or the pedophile wolves."

He laughs before grabbing my hand, squeezing it. "Well, things worked out just fine."

They have, haven't they? ...How many women did he sleep with, though?

"Tell me about you," he hedges, severing the jealousy threatening to eat at me before it begins. "When were you turned?"

I fidget behind him. If my palms could sweat, they would've started to. Guess we would have eventually gotten to this discussion, so why not just get it over with now... lay everything out? "I was turned in the thirties by a vampire who fancied me, even in my dirty, patchwork hand-me-downs." I wince, remembering that day. "I'd just lost my mother. I spent the entire day begging for change so I could scrounge up enough to afford her medicine. We worked at a sewing factory, the two of us, but she'd been let go when she became ill." I swallow back the lump beginning to form in my throat, hoping that will also stop the piercing pain starting in my chest. "Anyway, by the time I got home in the evening, she'd succumbed to pneumonia. I'd lost all three of my brothers within the five years prior to that, one of them just a few months before her passing. I left home that night and wandered the streets some more, not wanting to be in the house with my mother... and that's when he saw me. I'd gone into the bar for warmth since it was December in Chicago. The bartender demanded I leave if I wasn't going to buy a drink, so I tucked my numb fingers into my holey pockets and went on my way. He followed me from the bar, the vamp who'd been sitting in a corner alone, watching me. He followed me straight home, where he fed me his blood and drained me. I expected death, you know. I'd prayed for it, you see... But when I awakened as something else, I was... disappointed. Stunned. I had no idea such beings existed. I'd thought him a psychopath, a serial killer even. But I soon got over the initial shock and accepted the card I'd been dealt. Unlike him, I never preyed on anyone or attempted to force one's hand. Like you, I was offered marriage. He wanted me to be his vampire bride." I laugh, remembering how absurd it'd sounded when he first propositioned me. The sound turns bitter as I recall what happened in the next week. "I turned him down. I didn't want to belong to him, this man who thought he already owned me simply because he'd stalked me and turned me. He claimed he'd given me a new start in life... quite literally, a new life. He even changed my name to Rose, saying it suited me better. But I only wanted freedom. When he became forceful one evening, threatening to take away the life he'd granted me, I took his head off using the busted bottle of his favorite whisky. It'd been... poetic." I sigh, ready to bring my story to an end. "And that's my tragic little tale."

Julian's hand had returned to the handlebar during my story so he could continue to steer his bike, but upon hearing the very last of my tale of being turned, he'd once again brought his hand to mine, squeezing it gently with his own. "I'm sorry any of that happened to you."

"All is well now," I say, squeezing his hand back before he returns to steering, lest we end up colliding with a tree off the side of the road. "Things have worked out just fine."

And they truly have. While I'd grown content with my vampiric life, I'd also yearned for nothing. Wanted for nothing. Now, I yearn again. I want again.

I can only pray that this newfound happiness with Julian isn't soon extinguished.

Chapter 8. A Lover & Protector

We've pulled into a spot near the entrance to the quaint Farmers Market Denise was last spotted working at. Out front, above the door, sits a large green apple with a bite taken out of it, revealing the inner cream-colored flesh. Cursive letters in red curve around the unbitten side of the fruit, reading: *Crisp*.

What can we expect from little Miss. Snitch? Will she even be here, or does she have wolves on her two-faced back keeping an eye out for her?

I remove my helmet and hang it from the handlebar before I approach the reflective glass windows, seeing my own uncertain expression while spotting one female cashier playing on her phone at the register she's occupying. One glance around the lot upon first pulling in, I knew there weren't many customers. It would seem the only two cars parked belong to staff members. Is the old grey number Denise's, or perhaps the newer red hatchback?

Julian leaves his helmet on and grabs my hand before entering the store. Denise won't recognize me, but without his helmet on, she'll spot Julian immediately and run. I just hope she doesn't catch his scent right away and run.

The cashier doesn't look up from her phone when the automatic glass doors open, announcing the arrival of customers. We do, however, get a nice drab "Welcome to Crisp, where everything's ripe and brings you bliss."

Bit of a lame phrase if you ask me, but I smile nonetheless and respond with a polite "Thank you".

An unintelligible mumble comes off her lips as she continues to stare down at her phone.

"I can tell she loves working here," I note to Julian, as we pass by the peaches.

He's focused, on a mission, and my sarcasm goes ignored as he tugs me through the store.

Just when I think Denise is M.I.A., someone asks us if we need anything: "Help you with something?"

Julian and I turn to see a man. Well, a wolf... standing with a small crate full of packaged white mushrooms between his hands.

"Lookin' for a friend," Julian answers. "Denise."

The wolf narrows his green eyes at Julian's helmet. "Is there a reason you're wearing a helmet in here?"

Julian grunts, "Hangover."

Now the wolf's eyes are on me. "Denise isn't here."

I plant a smile on my face, hoping kindness gets me somewhere. "Know where we can find her?"

He looks at Julian again, not a twitch of a smile on his lips. "Nope."

On each side of the crate, his hands clench the wood. He's nervous... he knows something.

"You sure?" I ask, narrowing my own gaze at him. "I know for a fact she'd love to see me."

Now rude, his tone clipped: "And you are?"

"An old friend."

He snorts, "Denise isn't exactly friends with vamps."

Another hater of the fang. I take a step forward, with Julian keeping close by as I do. "I happen to know she does business with vamps... like the High Society. Heard of it?"

He gulps, and a bead of sweat glides slowly along the side of his bronze neck.

"She might've mentioned them before," he answers, voice now lower.

Still smiling, my tone sweet yet threatening, I say, "Then you know this matter is urgent, and I require her attention."

He looks between us again before he sets the crate down on the generic white tiles. "Follow me, then."

Julian gets ahead of me, his stance protective, as we follow this wolf to the back of the store, past double doors and through plastic covering another frame, straight into a storage area full of crates.

"She left this for you," the wolf calmly says, bending forward, his back to us.

When he turns around, he swings a large metal tool in the air, missing Julian's helmet by mere inches. Julian, having dodged the blow, grabs the end of what appears to be a crate opener and pulls the wolf forward, his hand now over his neck. He yanks the tool from the wolf's hand and shoves the sharp end straight into his abdomen. The wolf screams out, his eyes glowing a brighter green as he reels from the excruciating pain of being skewered so mercilessly.

"Tell me where that bitch is!" Julian growls, shoving the injured wolf into the nearest wall, the tool burying itself into his stomach deeper.

An unpleasant scream of pain emerges from the wolf once again, but he glares with illuminated, half-lidded eyes at Julian, brows set in anger above them. "Never telling you shit, rapist."

"Rapist?!" Julian asks, yanking his helmet off and throwing it on the floor. He stares eye-to-eye with the other wolf now. "That what she told you?"

He narrows his eyes at Julian, his feelings of disgust toward him obvious as he sneers. "Yeah, she told me all about you."

Julian huffs, stunned just as much as I am by her lie. "Let's get one thing straight: I ain't never forced myself on anyone. Denise betrayed her pack, got 'em all slaughtered. As the pack leader and guy who got tortured thanks to her, I'm lookin' to settle the score."

For a moment, the wolf's black brows pull up, his widened eyes telling of how unaware he is of what Denise has really done. She'd created an elaborate story about Julian hurting her to gain this man's trust and protection.

But soon, his brows set once more in anger as he eyes Julian. "You're lying." He looks at me. "And she told me all about the High Society of vamps and how you tortured *her* for days just for kicks."

I can only sadly shake my head. She'd been the one to aid in Julian being tortured, not the other way around as she'd painted it for this naïve wolf. "She was never touched. She's spun an entire web of lies to you. Don't you see? She needed protection, and she's clearly done all she can to ensure it, including feeding you ridiculous lies."

"I'm the one who got tortured," Julian growls. "Because of her deceit."

The wolf looks between us again, undecided now on who to believe.

"Look, we don't want to hurt you," I offer, hoping he'll cooperate. My eyes drift to where Julian's currently keeping a tool buried in his gut. "...You swung the crate opener first, you know. We just want Denise. Tell us where she is, and we'll leave you be."

Blood and spit spews from his mouth as he hangs his head and laughs, the mixture of the two falling to the grey cement at his feet in a swirl of tiny bubbles. His laughter soon ceases, but he doesn't raise his head.

"Fuck you," he finally says.

Not the answer I'd been hoping for. Julian isn't going to be pleased, and I can only imagine what he has planned for this guy to get him to talk.

Voice low, Julian leans in closer to him: "You sure you wanna protect someone who's only gonna betray you? Hell, she already has by tellin' you bullshit and puttin' you in danger with us."

"She's only ever loved me," he answers, head still down, bloodied mucus still dripping from his lips onto the floor.

Julian sighs in disappointment. "Hope she's worth what's comin'."

"Julian," I protest. "He's not going to talk."

He keeps his eyes on the wolf, his lip curling. "I can make him."

"That's what I'm afraid of." If he does this, he'll be sinking low. He'll be less than who I know him to be. "Surely there's another way."

He finally makes eye contact with me, his eyes telling of desperation. "If we let him go without gettin' the information we need, he'll go straight to Denise. She'll run again, and we'll lose her."

He's not wrong. My gut simply aches with the pain I know this wolf will soon face, all because his loyalty is misplaced... and because he clearly loves her. He's fallen for a lie.

"She's only using you," I plead with the wolf, now even more sympathetic toward him. "You have to see that now."

He lifts his head slowly, looking at me, blood dribbling down his chin. "All I see is a sociopath and a tramp vamp."

Taken aback by his words, I physically react, taking an actual step back.

Julian twists the metal tool in his gut, making him scream again. I take a couple steps back from the shock of Julian's action and the piercing scream of a man being tortured. I picture Julian chained to that metal table back at the mansion, imagining how he'd likely screamed the same as he'd been hurt over and over again.

"Julian, please," I beg. His nose wrinkles under his furrowed brows as his nostrils flare, blood beginning to coat his hand from how deep he's pushed the tool into the wolf's gut. "Stop this. He's only protecting someone he loves. He can't see who she really is."

"He's made his choice."

My hands form fists at my sides. "And you have a choice, too!"

Julian looks at me again, the glow that'd begun to brighten his blue-green irises fading as he watches me.

My anger softens, releasing my brows from their tightly knitted stance on my forehead. My fists unclench. "Please? This doesn't feel right."

He inhales deeply while he stares at me, before he grumbles and swiftly pulls the tool from the wolf's stomach, leaving him to fall to the floor with another scream. Julian tosses the crate opener into a corner of the room, the metal clinking loudly as it settles on the floor.

Without looking at me, Julian grabs his helmet from the floor and walks past me, back through the plastic and into the other room.

"Julian?" I ask, nearly bumping into him when he halts suddenly.

"What?!"

I can't help but jump in response to his unexpected, angered outburst. My voice is small with how on edge I am, uncertain of how he'll continue to act in response to me begging him to have mercy: "I just..."

He turns around, his anger visible beneath his glowing gaze. But his tone isn't so much angry as it is desperate and saddened: "I did what you asked. I left him be. Now we got nothin'. No leads, not jack shit." He gestures toward the plastic, where the wolf still resides behind it. "He'll run off and tell her we were here. She'll run again. What are we gonna do? Chase her forever? We had a chance back there to find her, and..." He rubs his brow with his unbloodied hand, closing his eyes as he begins to pinch the bridge of his nose.

"This isn't the way," I say, my voice lowering even more. "Don't you remember what they did to you? Do you want to become like them?"

He stops pinching his nose to look at me again, his eyes softening but his jaw clenching. "I'm nothin' like them."

"Maybe not now," I say, stepping closer, staring right up at him with conviction. "But keep this up, and you'll be getting closer and closer." I touch his arm, leaning closer. "I don't want that for you."

His shoulders slump as his rigid posture relaxes, his eyes heavily focused on mine. "I'm sorry."

"Don't be. Just don't... don't let her turn you into a shadow of who you are."

A smile tugs at the corners of his mouth. "When I've got an angel like you sittin' on my shoulder? I doubt she'll ever win that battle." His smile disappears. "I'm sorry for snappin' at you, too."

I shrug. "You lost yourself for a moment. It happens."

Shuffling from behind me interrupts us. Julian steps in front of me, shielding me from the wolf who's coming our way.

Emerging from behind the plastic, the wolf comes out, his hand splayed across the bloodied, ripped fabric of his cream-colored work tee. Defeat in his voice, he says: "She's at my barn."

Did he just tell us where we can find Denise? ...Why tell us now?

Julian shuffles his feet, probably just as uncertain of this guy's motives as I am. "...What?"

"My barn," he repeats, seeming impatient. "She's hiding out there."

Julian remains stiff, claws out, suspicion on his sleeve. "You were so set on protectin' her before. Why tell us now where she's at?"

The wolf inhales deeply before he answers: "Because if what you say is true, I gotta protect my own pack from her."

Chapter 9. Snitches End up in Ditches

Worried this could be a trap we're headed into, I've asked Julian to call for backup, but he's insisted that he handle Denise on his own. My suggestion of involving our friends was immediately dismissed.

"Dorian's got a baby and a wife to worry about," he'd argued.

"And Derick and Hailey?"

"Busy runnin' Vudu."

I'd rolled my eyes so dramatically, my head had fallen back. Hailey's been working with me, but I suppose he knows Derick would never allow her to go on a dangerous mission without him.

But still I argue: "This wolf's pack could be occupying the barn as we speak. She could be *in* the pack!" Oh, I hadn't even thought of that till now, her joining a new pack she can just destroy later. I'd just thought she was romantically (and deceitfully) involved with one of its members. If my hands weren't so firmly wrapped around Julian as I balance myself behind him on his bike, I'd have begun biting my nails.

"I've got this, trust me."

What is it with wolves always wanting to do everything the macho way? "It's okay to ask for help from time to time, you know."

"I've got all the help I need right here."

Right, a vampire like me can totally destroy a pack of wolves. "And if there are, say, at least ten wolves waiting for us there? I'll be dismembered in minutes."

Julian's spine straightens. "You're right..." He slows and pulls over on the side of the road. "Best if I do this alone."

He can't be serious! And he's what? Leaving me on the side of the road?! "No way!"

"You're right – it's too dangerous for you."

"If you think I'm getting off this bike, Julian Napper, you'll have to—"

"Carry you off?" he finishes, standing up with my arms still wrapped around his torso, lifting my behind off the seat as he does.

I refuse to let go, though, stubbornly holding him tight around his shoulders now while he maneuvers himself off his bike. "I'm not leaving you to face off with that psycho wretch and her clueless claw-wielding friends!" I lift myself higher, tightening my legs around his waist next.

He gently tugs at my arms and legs from where they refuse to budge around his neck and torso. "Better I get hurt than you."

I just tighten them more. "What kind of mentality is that! We're supposed to be in this fight together."

"The kind that says you're my mate, and I ain't riskin' you gettin' hurt... or dismembered!"

"That's right! We're mates! I forbid you to galivant off and get killed!"

He stops fooling with my arms and slouches, momentarily giving up with a sigh. "Ivy..."

"No!" I refuse to allow him to even think that I'd ever be okay with him leaving me stranded while he runs off to put himself in harm's way. "I might be a vamp, but I can still handle myself. If you're this adamant about going after her right this moment with absolutely no backup other than myself, then I'm going with you. End of discussion."

Another sigh.

Still, I hold him tightly. Can't let my guard down just yet. As soon as I do, he'll overpower me... won't he?

"You really think she'll be alone?" I ask him.

"I don't know."

"Guess we'll find out."

He grunts before getting on his bike. "We'll just stop and have a look. If she's not alone, I'll be able to tell."

His nose is far more powerful than mine. Not to mention, wolves have heartbeats, making them easier to detect if you listen for them.

As Julian settles himself back on his bike, I slide my legs away from his waist, adjusting myself behind him cautiously. I still wonder if he'll end up tossing me off his bike and speeding off without me if he thinks he's doing right by me in doing so.

But he doesn't. We ride out to a vacant area, the dirt from the old road spinning under our tires and billowing out behind us in giant swirling clouds. Ahead, there's a large barn with peeling white paint all over it, the kind you'd find horses in. As we near it, I can't hear anything over Julian's engine. So much for trying to pick up beating hearts.

He stops near the edge of where the barn sits, cutting his engine. "She's alone."

Over the light breeze jostling the full trees on the land, their leaves tickling one another joyously, a single racing heart beats away in the distance. She might be alone, but judging from her panicked heart, she knows we're here. I spot a black tarp covering a vehicle off to the side of the barn, its shiny new tires showing.

I say nothing as Julian gets off his bike. While I can hear her, she won't hear me. Instead of following him to the barn, I signal with my fingers that I'll be by her car. Julian nods before he removes his helmet, and I run off like the predator I am, my flats silent as they race across the grass and gravel. I disappear from his sight just as quickly as he's gone from mine. Removing my helmet, I lift the tarp and try the handle of the backseat door. As it fully clicks, releasing, I open it just enough to slide into the backseat. If Julian finds himself in peril, I'll sense it from him and can just as quickly aid him. But if Denise manages to evade him and attempts to leave, I'll be waiting for her...

And the little pocket knife I've pulled from my crossbody bag will be just the weapon I'll use on her before she gets the chance to claw me to death. Granted, I'm strong as well and can rip her head off... but she has claws. Strength-wise, she can best me. I have to be quicker... predatory... prepared.

From where I'm hiding on the cramped floor of her little red Range Rover, a shiver radiates up my spine, just as Julian screams. I twitch, prepared to leave my station, but I know he's not terribly wounded – just hurt. Irritated. Angry.

And then I hear it – the sound of shoes hitting gravel forcefully as someone runs... getting closer and closer. Sunlight filters into the car through the windows as the tarp is yanked free from the vehicle. The driver's side door opens, and Denise settles into the seat, grabbing the keys left in the ignition and turning them just as quickly as her door has closed.

That's when I pounce. Before she can drive off, her hand on the clutch, I rise from the backseat, knife in hand, and stab her through the neck. As she's bleeding and screaming, eyes widened and mouth open with garbled gasps as she watches me in the rearview mirror, I push the knife in deeper.

I don't want to kill her. I'd simply wanted to stun her, to render her helpless for Julian to do what he needed to do with her.

And she knows that, my hesitation to do anything more than stab her apparent. Raised, shocked brows soon pull down as she eyes me. Those claws make an appearance as she begins to slash them toward me, cutting my arms and leaving me to yell out now. Wolf bites are the worst, but being shredded comes second.

Eventually, I must move back to protect myself, and just as soon as I have, the backdoor opens, and I'm grabbed by my arm and yanked out of the car. The wolf from Crisp is there, pulling me up before my arms have even healed from Denise's claw marks, holding me up by my throat, my feet dangling and flats coming off as I kick my legs.

Under his grip, I can't even call for Julian.

I knew things would end this way, that Julian's thirst for revenge would eventually lead to my demise. Being with him had been dangerous, and becoming his mate had only increased my odds of ending up ash. But I'd only wanted him. Loved him. I'd willingly made such a sacrifice for the chance to be loved back.

And I'd do it all over again.

Even under this wolf's strangling grip, as I look into green eyes glowing vibrantly under the afternoon sun, I know that much.

I just hope Julian makes it out alive.

"You can't kill her that way," Denise announces, having summoned the strength after healing to exit the vehicle and come near in her bloodied flannel shirt and cut-off jean shorts. "Damn vamps don't breathe."

For a moment, as he looks between me and her, I see hesitation in his eyes. His grip even loosens. "Let's just go. We can run together."

"I don't wanna run anymore, Landon. I want them dead."

He sighs in agitation before he lets go of me, leaving me to fall back to the earth, the rocks making up the gravel digging into my bare knees, pricking me painfully. I bring a trembling hand to my throat, the pain from his death grip subsiding already.

"What are you doing?!" she shouts.

"Tell me the truth," he demands. "Did you get your last pack slaughtered? Your leader tortured?"

A low laugh escapes Denise. "So, they told you, huh?"

I look up at Landon, then Denise, a sneer on her face as she regards him. His hands clench at his sides, claws elongating into his dark skin, the puncture wounds beginning to bleed and drip onto the dried grass.

"You said he raped you," Landon says through clenched teeth.

She rolls her eyes. "You believed what you wanted to believe."

"I believed what you told me!"

"And if I'd said I was on the run for outing my pack to vamps just to save my own ass... you would've taken me in still?"

He shifts his feet.

"That's what I thought," she says, eyeing him with a blank expression. Then she looks at me. "Well if you're not gonna off this bitch, I am."

Landon moves in front of where I sit.

Deep lines form on Denise's forehead as her brows come up. "You're gonna protect a fuckin' vamp over me now?" she asks him.

"You lied to me."

"Oh get the fuck over it!" she exclaims, laughing, her head rolling back with her eyes. She tears her eyes from the sky above, one that's become overcast, staring at Landon now. "Our pack asked for what they got the moment they chose to go against a society of vampires! And Julian..." She gestures toward the barn. "He allowed it. Them getting torn apart was his fault! He should've protected *us*, worried about our own kind! But no, he wanted to help out his friends and involved us in their shit! So I did what I had to do!"

"You could've sided with your pack!" he yells at her. "That's what you do when you join one. You're family. You don't just surrender them all and betray them!"

She snorts. "Don't act so noble. You'd have done the same thing."

He shakes his head. "No! I wouldn't have."

She looks between us. "So now what, Landon? You gonna kill me?"

"No..." He nods toward where Julian has appeared in the doorway of the barn. "I'm leaving you to your leader."

Eyes now wide, Denise turns around quickly, claws out.

I'm relieved Julian's okay, but judging from his reddened skin and soaked cotton tee, she'd doused him with aconite. That'd been the reason for his scream.

When Landon begins to walk away, the sound of his boots crunching over the gravel, Denise turns to see him retreating.

"You're gonna leave me to them?!" she shouts. "So much for love, huh?!"

Landon stops abruptly before he slowly turns to face her again. "You wanna go there with me? I know about Maverick."

"I... He was just there... It just happened. He... we—"

Landon cuts her off: "You slept with him. You didn't even think about me! Mav said you were drunk, that he was too. But that didn't matter, did it? You slept with him because you have no loyalty to anyone!"

She lets out another laugh, one that sounds bitter. "I never claimed to be perfect." Now jabbing a finger toward Landon, she raises her voice: "*You* chose to put me on a pedestal, to think I was some poor, innocent, damaged bitch!"

Landon slowly shakes his head as he eyes her with sympathy. "I thought you were just in a bad frame of mind, that you needed to heal inside. You lied to me. As it turns out, you just don't give a fuck about anybody. You never loved me. You've been using me. ...And you've screwed me over for the last time." He looks at Julian, who's stalking toward Denise. "She's all yours."

I stand up just as Julian's reached her. All I can do is watch as he grabs her throat and chokes her, his claws digging into her neck, blood spewing out from the wounds. She struggles under his grip, clawing at his face and neck, all the while desperately attempting to breathe under his hold, small sounds making their way out of her.

Julian's eyes are bright with his rage as he watches her die.

And mine are filled with terror. Not for her. For him.

"Stop!" I scream, rushing toward them, grabbing at his hand around her throat.

Julian tries to ignore me, but just as his eyes dim, his resolve to kill her wavering, he lets her go, her body weakly falling to the ground.

Voice filled with regret, he murmurs: "Dammit, Ivy."

"I can't let you do this," I tell him, urging him back with my palms on his chest, away from her. "I can't let you kill her. It'll change you."

"I've killed before."

"Like this?" I ask, cool tears streaming down my cheeks.

His brows pull in as he watches me, a certain unease forming in his eyes. "...No."

"Maybe we *should* let her go," I whisper, only wanting us to have a peaceful future, one that isn't tainted by today, if he goes through with killing her as punishment. This is a defining moment for us, one that will shape our entire future.

He looks at Denise, who's holding her throat and coughing still as she lies on the ground. "If I let her go, she could find us later... and she won't be so kind to us."

He's right. Dammit, he's right.

I look down at his shirt, a wetness under my palms from where he still burns because she'd thrown aconite on him. ...She's out for herself, always has been. And she'd told Landon she wants us dead. She doesn't want to run anymore. "I know."

Now that Denise has gathered her bearings, she stands up, her back to us. "And I will... I'll find you. I'll never stop coming, not after this. I'll fuck you and kill you!" She turns around, eyes glowing a bright yellow, two clawed fingers pointing at me. "And then I'll fuck your dead girlfriend before I shred her pretty little face and cut her head clean off!"

I've turned around slowly hearing her threats, how her voice had gone from raised to screaming, my mouth open in disgust hearing her threatening words.

She laughs at me, her eyes finding Julian's next. "Actually, I think I'll let you watch me fuck her and kill her first."

A growl emerges from her, just before Julian lunges at her, grabbing her throat and ripping her head off before she can even think to defend herself.

As her remains fall to the bloodied brown grass, the once stunning blades just as dead as she now is, Julian tosses her head near her ravaged neck.

All I can do is stare at her corpse, a churning beginning in my gut, a slice of pain piercing through my chest. I don't mourn this monster's death. I mourn what it might do to Julian.

Chapter 10. Girl Talk

Following Denise's death, Julian submerged himself in investigating the murders of blondes in surrounding counties. The latest victim? Annabelle Levy, a twenty-year old last spotted leaving work in our very own city, just a block from where I now sit doing inventory.

Did I not just order an entire box of edible panties? I turn to Hailey. "Did we sell all those edible britches already?"

She stands there holding a black lace chemise she'd just been about to hang up along with others, her hazel eyes looking up in thought. "I sold several pairs last week to one gentleman in particular."

Several pairs, huh? Must've been stocking up. "Guess I'll order more."

My thoughts wander back to the killer within moments. The other victims have been blonde as well. That seems to be the only similarity between them all. Some were tan, others pale. Some thin, others average or voluptuous. Even their eye colors didn't match; some had blue, others brown or green. But all of them had the same natural blonde hair. Their bodies all go missing without a trace. And whoever this sicko is always texts those who contact the phone of each victim with the same message: *Met the love of my life and moved to Mexico. TTYN!*

Poor Madison had been subjected to the same evil, but she'd fortunately survived. I can't say the same for the other girls, which sends an ache through my chest every time I allow myself to think about them.

We can't allow this serial killer to remain on the loose. All my efforts have been futile, dead ends meeting me for months now. I was a pro at tracking vamps for decades, but this one... he's different. Smarter. Slicker. Creepier. Was he a killer as a human, too? There's darkness in him, but I suspect it's always been there... even before he was turned.

While Julian might be using this search and investigation as a coping mechanism, a distraction for killing Denise, I'm grateful for his dedication to finding and ending this killer's reign. Maybe he'll have better luck than me. Unlike Denise, this is one individual I won't mind executing. Denise had been motivated by fear and selfishness, by her primal instincts to survive no matter what, not even if it meant handing over her pack to the High Society. But this psychotic vampire delights in controlling and draining his victims, relishing their final screams. He stashes their bodies God only knows where. He isn't looking out for himself or surviving. No, he's enjoying himself and the pain he causes each and every girl he takes.

"Sold that same guy a lot of dildo's, too," Hailey comments suddenly, while she continues to hang lingerie. "Wonder what he's doing with all of it..."

I quirk a single brow at her. "Having sex..."

She pauses hanging a chemise to look at me, a smile forming across her pink glossy lips. "Smart-ass."

I giggle before resuming the tedious task I'd been only partially invested in. Scattered thoughts about Julian and that killer have left me consistently unfocused.

"Hmmm," Hailey hums, seduction in her tone, getting my attention once again. In her hand, she's holding a lacey hot pink corset. "Ever worn something like this for Julian?"

Since sex was last had on the very floor Hailey now stands, the carpet replaced after Julian and I had ripped it up to hide the evidence of two dead wolves, Julian and I haven't engaged in such a riveting act since. It's been a solid four days since we'd bonded. I haven't had the pleasure of seducing him. "Not yet..."

She grins, dangling the corset. "Might I suggest you wear it, then?" She holds up a matching thong next, twirling the string around her index finger. "And this to match."

My loins tingle in anticipation, lighting a familiar fire within me as I think about wearing such skimpy attire for Julian. I imagine his pleased reaction, his eyes lazily wandering from the top of the pink corset framing my breasts, making them spill over the tightly bound cups – to the cinched waist and triangular end of the very thong Hailey's twirling around her finger. His hands, hot and callused, will send jolts of fiery electricity everywhere they touch, from the side of my neck, around the dip of my collarbone, over my emphasized breasts, down my waist, over my rump... the tips of his rough fingers teasing at the soft and delicate skin of my backside.

I nearly drop the pen in my hand, my grip having loosened on it.

Hailey's grin widens as she observes my sudden jellied reaction. Hmm... if I get something for myself, it's only right she does as well. I point the ink-end of my pen at her. "I'll buy all that if you get something, too."

She laughs and grabs a silky black chemise. "Already one step ahead of you." After putting it against her front and looking down to admire it, she sets it back down and focuses next on the empty boxes at her feet, a small sigh making its way out. "Guess I'll go get those other boxes now. The sooner I finish stocking, the quicker I can get home to Derick."

As she heads off to the storage room in the basement (a separate room from my living quarters below), I stare down at the inventory papers once again, then back up at the computer. Then my eyes drift toward the few boxes Hailey had just unpacked. I'd rather stock than do inventory, so I set the papers aside and tear my eyes from the computer screen. I can't focus anyway.

She's mostly unpacked everything, save for some beads and whips set aside. I bend down and retrieve the box of beads before heading toward where they're normally stocked. As I'm hanging them, thinking of wearing that lingerie for Julian, picturing his mouth hanging open... a door slams, causing me to jump.

Hailey screams, the type of bloodcurdling sound that sends chills over one's figure. Mine is currently overcome by them, goosebumps spreading along my arms, raising the fine hairs.

I drop the box with a thump against the new red carpet (pink was so last year), the packaged beads protesting as they clink against each other, and run toward the hall. The storage room door is closed. I try the black knob, but it won't budge, which is odd since there's no lock.

I pound my palm against the painted black wood. "Hailey!"

Over her panicked screams, what sounds like boxes being kicked over and items falling from the metal shelves panics me further.

"Hailey!" I scream again, finally stepping back and kicking the door in with the bottom of my black MaryJane.

That's when the lights flicker in the basement, turning back on, lighting up the wooden steps leading down.

"The hell?" I mutter, observing clutter everywhere along the cement floor from where things had fallen off the shelves. I take a few steps down, looking for Hailey. "What happened?"

Hailey comes barreling around the corner downstairs, a skidded knee already healing, straight up the steps toward me like a madwoman. Eyes crazed, dark wavy hair an absolute mess, she nearly knocks me over grabbing me to haul me out of the basement, too.

Something terrorized her, but what? Who?

"Who's down there?" I demand, attempting to push past her to go back down.

"No!" she begs, frightening me now.

"What happened?" I ask her again, waiting while I watch her settle down, her hands rubbing the tops of her bare arms anxiously.

Her voice is shaky: "Remember how we talked about ghosts at the fairgrounds?"

The night we'd ended the High Society for good, Hailey had brought up spirits. I'd given my two cents on the subject, telling her how ghosts had to exist when creatures like vamps and wolves wandered around. Over the decades, I'd also heard stories of other dimensions beyond our reach.

"...Yeah," I answer. Is she saying a ghost was down there with her? She's shaking, her still wide eyes on the open basement door. I touch her hands, stilling her movement of rubbing them up and down. "My goodness, you're all out of sorts."

Her eyes begin to glisten as she stares into mine. She opens her mouth, her glossed lips trembling, before she closes it, clearly uncertain of what words to say. But finally, after I've patiently waited for her to go on, she says, "...Claire's been haunting me."

Claire had been a friend and roommate to Hailey, before she was viciously murdered by Sal, one of Catherine's guards in the High Society. I'd nearly fainted myself upon seeing Claire's scattered body parts and blood spattered across the walls and carpet in the apartment she used to share with Hailey. How anyone could do something so horrific is beyond me, and in all my decades of being undead, I'd never seen anything so gruesome, so heartless and evil. Hailey had seen the same horrific sight, but Claire was someone she knew well and cared about. Finding someone you're close with like that... knowing they died at the hands of a vampire that might as well have been a demon... I can't even imagine the pain she feels. But why would Claire be haunting Hailey?

"Haunting you?" I ask.

She nods again. "It's like she's getting stronger. Like... like she wants my attention, but I don't know what for." She closes her eyes, tears slowly gliding down the faint pink of her cheeks. "Maybe she hates me."

Hailey's one of the kindest souls I've ever met. Someone hating her would be like me hating blood... very unnatural. "I very much doubt that."

"You don't understand," she begins to weep. "I left her with little to no explanation, and not long after, she was murdered. She blames me."

Hailey had left her apartment to go on the run from the High Society not long before Claire was targeted. The whole point of leaving was to not only protect herself, but to protect Claire from the deadly supernatural world she knew nothing of. "You left her to protect her."

Eyes still closed, her pain obvious as more tears begin to escape them, she lowers her head. "All I did was sign her death slip."

I shake my head, unwilling to believe Claire blames someone as warm-hearted as Hailey for her murder. I firmly hold her shoulders beneath my palms. "That can't be it." Hailey thinks she wants her attention, right? "You said she wants your attention."

"She must, to keep showing up." She opens her eyes, though they only stare down at her red velvet boots. "Sometimes I awaken at night hearing her crying my name."

My heart aches for both her and Claire. I step closer, wrapping my arms around Hailey, giving her the best comfort I can when words aren't enough. If Claire wants Hailey's attention, we have to find out why. "If she wants to talk, we must reach out."

She sniffles. "How?"

"Wix."

"What's that?"

I step back, letting go of her shoulders. "A sort of... magic shop up the strip."

She lifts her eyes, revealing how red they'd become, as she watches me curiously. "...A magic shop?"

It's not exactly a magic shop, but she'll see soon enough. "We'll need a Ouija board."

In Wix, Hailey looks around the shop with intrigue, her focus moving from one unfamiliar thing to the next. On standing shelves made of dark-stained wood are jars containing dried herbs, feathers, petals, etc. – their labels detailing their type and purpose (most are for spells or protection). Lotions made from natural ingredients sit side-by-side in clear plastic bottles. Chunky candles are stacked together while the long, skinny ones are in wicker baskets, all separated by color and purpose. Books line other shelves against a wall, their contents containing spells and potions, all ranging from beginner to experienced. Natural stones meant for healing purposes or other uses fill glass bowls. Beaded jewelry including necklaces, bracelets and anklets dangle from black velvet holders. Metal rings are fastened on fingers of hands made of black velvet as well. Some rings are made of sterling, gold or rose gold, some are simple bands with details carved on them, others with raw and jagged stones atop them as opposed to the polished ones you'd find in other shops. Their tags claim their hand-made by the owner, Velda, and I know this to be true. Most everything in this shop is hand-made, including the stained-glass wind chimes and beaded suncatchers at the front of the shop near the large windows. I've always admired the way the crystals and glass beads catch the sunlight and send rainbow-colored sparkles across the walls and shelves.

I've been to Wix several times before to purchase Velda's soaps and lotions, as I enjoy the light and natural scents of them, particularly the vanilla lavender or citrus sage. Having imagined her as an older woman with long white hair travelling past the middle of her back in haphazard waves and a shawl around her shoulders and pointed black boots on her feet, I was surprised to find she was young, not quite twenty-five the first time we actually met. Her style is more boho – I've seen her mostly wearing floral maxi dresses with ankle boots or jeans with flowy tops that accentuate her curvaceous figure. She often wears her short black hair down, the almost straight strands of her bangs sometimes hanging over her eyes (that's why the occasional clips hold them back when she's busy stocking or running around the shop assisting customers).

The jewelry she makes herself always dangles from her neck and wrists, and several rings adorn her fingers. I've noticed her favorite stone is labradorite. Whether that's because it's her birth month or because she likes the green, blue and gold colors swirled within the stone, I'm not sure. We haven't conversed much, but that's because Velda knows I'm not human. She often cautiously rings me up at the front, her heart beating faster, her hands shaking as she works to scan the tags of items I've selected, as she's shakily placed all purchased merchandise in the little black paper bags. I'm fond of the design of the bags: plain save for an icon of a lit white candle on the front, the Wix name a halo around the top of the flame. Given her fear of me, I've wondered why she doesn't turn me away. Perhaps she fears me biting into her and letting her bleed out if she denies me service. Vamps have an awful reputation, and witches steer clear if they can.

I wander to the back of the shop where I've seen the Ouija boards before, looking down aisles for Velda or her employees as I do. She usually has help – a couple younger girls who assist in the shop to stock or run the register. Velda's protective of them. Though she fears me, she never lets the other workers ring me up. Once, she even came up front as I was prepared to make my purchase, telling the girl she needed some lavender candles re-stocked. Prior to me walking up to the register, I'd just passed by the candle shelf, and the lavender candles had been well-stocked. She'd wanted to keep her staff safe from the blood-sucking vamp...

I catch sight of one of the girls I've seen a few times before. She's rearranging oils on a shelf, her focus unwavering as she completes the task. She hasn't seen me yet. If she had, I would've heard it in her frenzied heartbeat. It currently beats steady and calm.

Now at the back of the store, I reach for a Ouija board box, one of three, and pull it from the shelf it'd been sitting on. Most boards you'd see are made by a toy company, but Velda's are hand-made, like most everything else here. As I look over the box, which shows an image of what is expected to be inside (the board, pointer thingie and instructions), I'm not at all surprised to see the price.

And Hailey sees it too, a gasp coming up her throat before she hisses near my ear: "Two-hundred dollars?!"

"It's hand-made," I defend with a shrug. I admire the carved letters pictured on the box, their color a dark brown against the caramel-colored board. "Look at those details."

"Still..."

I edge away from the shelf. "Let's check out, shall we?"

As we walk past the girl handling small jars of oils, she looks up to smile at us, to greet us. But as soon as she sees us, a couple of vamps exuding our unnatural and deadly vibes, the greeting I'd expected never comes. Her mouth just hangs open, and the smile she'd had begins to fade just as quickly as it'd come on. Ah, there's that warming welcome I just knew would come as soon as she saw me. I vaguely register her nametag: Mindy.

At the empty register, Hailey whispers: "What was that about? She was... scared."

Of course she was. "She knows what we are. Vamps have a bad rep, remember?"

Disappointment clearly shows in her knitted brows. "Oh... right."

Guess she forgot about that.

A cheerful yet modestly shaky *Hello* now greets us from Velda. I recognize her voice before I've seen her. She walks confidently up to the counter and makes eye contact with the two of us, her mascara-coated lashes long and thick around her piercing blues. Today, she's wearing a light grey dress that hugs her curves and a dark blue jean jacket. Her hair is up in a perfect bun, not a single hair out of place.

She looks at the board I'd set down on the counter, confusion crossing her features. "Having a séance, are we?"

"We have a bit of a ghost sitch," I admit, explaining why two undead vamps are about to reach out to the totally dead.

Velda actually laughs as her icy blues dart between us, something I find odd since she usually just avoids eye contact with me and barely utters the total after she's rang me up. She shakes her black bangs out of her eyes, clears her throat and begins to lose her amused smile as she registers our confused expressions. "Really? Anyone you know or just a malevolent spirit?"

Hailey shrinks into herself slightly. "A friend."

What's left of Velda's smile fades into seriousness as she regards Hailey, noticing the change in her posture, the way her eyes have slipped away from Velda's and now rest on the counter. "I'm sorry for your loss."

Hailey glances at her. "Thanks."

Velda bites her naked bottom lip, her hesitation to ring us up obvious as she holds the board while watching us, her eyes flitting from me to the other vamp at my side. "Um... well... did you want to reach out to this friend just to check on them? Because if they're at peace, it's much more difficult to receive a response."

"Not exactly," I answer. "This spirit has been trying to give Hailey a message." I look at Hailey, stepping just an inch closer toward her. "We need to find out what that message is." For all we know, Claire's in some kind of trouble, her cries for Hailey in the middle of the night possibly pleads for help.

"I see..."

I look at Velda once more. Her brows have pulled in, showing off the line between them. Her eyes are still on me. Silence drags on between us as we stare at one another.

"Is something wrong?" I ask her.

She inhales sharply and blinks herself away from my curious gaze. "...No." She grabs the hand-held scanner and promptly scans the box, announcing the total, making Hailey cringe before she reaches into her purse.

"I've got this," I quickly tell Hailey, grabbing my own wallet from inside my small crossbody. This was my idea, after all, and I'd chosen Wix to ensure we got a legit board, which also ensured a steeper price.

Hailey tilts her head to the side, her eyes creasing worriedly as she watches me pull my card out. "Are you sure?"

"Of course." I smile, handing Velda my silver plastic card.

She takes it without caution, the tip of her finger even touching mine for a moment. It's then that I realize her heart is steady, the beat not quickened and under stress as it normally is in my presence. What's changed between us? Why isn't she... afraid of me?

Chapter 11. Séance

We'd left Vixen unattended and locked up at thirty till midnight before we'd walked the strip to get to Wix. Closing early so often probably is bad for business, but we've got bigger problems. Sex will never cease to sell, and since things generally slow down between twelve and two, I'm not at all worried about losing customers.

Now back at Vixen, after I've opened the basement door, Hailey protests: "Wait, we're not going down *there* to do this... are we?"

I turn back to see her twiddling her thumbs in front of her. "It's the last place she was. It only makes sense..."

She looks at the open door for a few moments before nodding once, giving me the okay to proceed. As we walk down the rickety steps, little creeks sounding out under our shoes, I see the mess I'll soon need to clean up waiting for me below. I can't help but dread having to pick up the clutter on the floor. My mind should be completely focused on Claire, but with bottles of lube, boxes of condoms and packaged penises scattered everywhere from Hailey's attempted escape, I can't help but become distracted. I'm not fond of messes.

And speaking of distractions, when I spot an opened box of lace panties, I think of Julian, who I can't wait to tell my extracurricular activities to. I wonder what he'll think of my undead-self reaching out to the dead-dead... Or what he'll think of the lingerie I plan to wear for him, probably tonight... he's due to stop by at two. I plan out my evening: séance first, followed by seducing Julian, then telling him how said séance went while we cuddle in bed post-mind-blowing-sex (no need to tell him *before* sex – that's much too distracting).

And how will this experimental séance business go? Will Claire answer us?

In the basement, past the clutter, I've set the box housing the Ouija board down on a small folding table.

"We'll need these," Hailey says, holding up the black candles Velda had recommended before we'd left Wix.

"Black candles offer the most protection from evil," Velda had said.

She was actually looking out for us, her natural arch nemeses? At least, I can only assume we are, given her past behavior toward me (clipped tone, eye contact avoidance, shaky fingers and racing heart). But she hadn't reacted that way tonight, and I'm still puzzled by that.

Hailey lights the candles using a silver penis-shaped lighter she'd grabbed from a box.

"I always thought black candles symbolized evil," I comment, attempting to open the Ouija box, noticing a large piece of tape holding it together. Had Velda lied, or are black candles really the most protective kind? "Guess I need to buy a book on symbolism in magic or whatever next."

Hailey, seeing me trying to carefully peel the tape back without damaging the box, grabs a box cutter off another shelf and holds it out for me to take. "Here, use this."

Unboxing things is my specialty down here, but I guess I'm a little nervous about what we're about to do; I hadn't even considered using a box cutter. I slide the blade across where the tape keeps the box lid on, the silver edge so sharp it cleanly makes its way through. I unbox the contents – the board, a pointer thingie and a piece of paper instructing us what to do. I read over everything quickly, as it's only a paragraph of actual instructions (the other details are warnings about opening gates one will need to close lest they want to be haunted and harmed till death do they and their spirit(s) part).

"Says to find a quiet and peaceful place where you can focus and hold the planchette over the board while you reach out to the spirit world," I announce, holding up the planchette tool I'd been thinking of as a pointer thingie. "Mentions holding it over *Hello* as we begin, as sort of a greeting."

Hailey snorts, "A greeting... sounds so polite considering how I've been haunted so disrespectfully." She then sighs, readying herself as she rolls her shoulders back, standing taller. "Let's get this over with."

Still holding the planchette, I look between her and the board. "One more thing."

"Yeah?"

"Only one person should be in control of the board. You want to do the honors, since you were close to her?"

Her brows pull down in worry. For several seconds, she's quiet, thinking through what she wants to do. "You're right – I should be the one to reach out."

I slowly hand her the planchette, and she takes it from me with a deep inward breath.

We settle ourselves into small plastic chairs with shiny metal legs at the table. The two black candles held within small glass jars flicker from our movements. I get a whiff of blackberry. "You think she's full of it?" I ask Hailey.

"What?"

"Velda..." I nod at the candles. "They're scented and in jars. Maybe she was just trying to make another sale."

Hailey grins before muttering, "Hope so..."

I study her, wondering what she means. "You hope so? Do you not want protection?"

Her focus is on the board, though she hasn't set the planchette down yet. "It's not that. I just hope none of this is real. I'm... scared."

I give her a smile. "Don't be. You know Claire best. She would never do anything to hurt you, right?"

Hailey's eyes quickly find mine, her expression hard. "I don't know that."

My smile falls. "Come again?"

She sighs. "Claire was..." She looks up, trying to finds words is my guess. "Awful sometimes." She shakes her head, her brows knitting. "A lot of times."

Now with eyes widened in surprise and confusion, and a mind telling me this likely isn't going to fare well if Claire was truly such an awful person, I glance at the board, about to call this whole thing off. "Um..."

"She wasn't always so horrible," Hailey immediately says, seeing my alarm. "She was just... shallow at times. Conceited. Rude. Lacked tact."

I look around the room, uneasy now myself. "Probably should've mentioned this before we got this far, don't you think? Not to mention, calling our subject shallow, conceited and tactless before contacting her seems... unwise."

"I'm just worried she's angry, that she blames me for her untimely demise. In death, she could be consumed by that anger, looking to hurt me."

Well, this certainly changes things. I huff, "Given the colorful description of her character you just described..."

Hailey fiddles with the planchette between her fingers, tapping it on the table. "She was more than those things. Despite all her flaws, she did have a good heart. She just had difficulty listening to it at times. She was young... and she wasn't given the chance to right her wrongs in life."

I let out a modest sigh. "Let's give her a chance, then. Maybe she only wants to say her peace."

"I hope so," Hailey agrees, finally holding the planchette over the *Hello* text. With a deep breath and a shaky voice, she says, "Hello... Claire." Tears begin to well in her eyes. "I miss you," she whispers. "I'm sorry for what happened."

With stiff shoulders and arms tightly bound across my front, I lean forward, watching the board, waiting for a response. My legs are just as stiff under me, thighs tightly held together, feet lifted as if I'm prepared to make a run for it.

At least if the lights go out (and the candles), I still have that penis lighter. Then again, I can see fine in the dark. It's the panic I might experience that worries me. I could end up like Hailey, who sees just as well in darkness, stumbling over lube bottles and dildos as I try to escape an angry spirit out to get revenge. I imagine myself sliding around in lube from bottles busted open under my stilettos, hitting my head on the bottom step of the stairs and being knocked unconscious.

Hailey jumps when the planchette moves, making me jump in my seat, too.

"Did you...?" I ask.

She keeps her eyes on the board. "No, it's not me."

I want to ask more, like if she feels anything, but I know I must be quiet and let her take the lead. Still patient, I wait... and the planchette twitches under Hailey's fingers, making her jump again. The more it twitches, the less she jumps, now expecting it to move. And it does. Slowly, decidedly, it roams across the board, finding four letters: S, A, M, E.

"She misses you, too," I declare with the lightest whisper I can. Shoulders now relaxing, thighs no longer clenched, I allow a calmness to fall over me. She's not mad, then. Good sign. ...Unless she's sorry for what happened to her as well and blames Hailey, and she's about to unleash hell on us as a result...

"Are you... okay?" Hailey asks.

The planchette moves to *NO*.

We both tense up again.

"Why not?" Hailey asks.

TRAPPED is spelled out next.

"She's in purgatory," I guess, a tightness forming in my chest. How dreadful.

Before Hailey can ask anything else, the planchette moves to *YES*, confirming my statement.

"Can you get out?" Hailey asks.

YES.

"How?"

TRIALS.

"Trials?" Hailey murmurs, not understanding.

I think quickly, attempting to search through decades of information in my mind. Trials... What could she mean? If she's in purgatory, and she can only escape it by going through trials, then those trials... those tests are meant to determine if she should pass through to the other side.

"She must complete tests in order to find the light," I tell Hailey.

The planchette moves to *YES.*

Hailey appears disturbed, her brows firmly planted in the same worried pose. "Is coming here part of your trials?"

NO.

The fine hairs on Hailey's arms raise with bumps along her skin. "Then... why are you here? I'm not complaining, Claire. I do miss you. I've just been... scared. Worried about you, also. Do you have a message for me?"

YES.

"What's the message?" I ask, forgetting I need to allow Hailey to be in charge. Too late, now. I've spoken.

Claire answers: *SORRY.*

"Sorry for what?" Hailey asks.

FAILED M.

"Failed M...," Hailey thinks aloud. "M... Madison?"

YES.

Chest now heavier, cool tears form behind my eyes, blurring the board. The night Madison was turned into a vampire, Claire had been with her and Hailey at Club Vudu. Hailey had seen Madison wander off with a man and had wanted to go after her, to make sure she was okay. But Claire had told her Madison was fine, to let her go. They later went home without Madison, and the man she'd helplessly wandered off with had been the vamp who'd killed and unintentionally turned her. Does Claire feel responsible for Madison's fate? Is that why she thinks she failed her?

"You didn't fail her," Hailey says, wiping tears away from her eyes with the back of one of her hands. "We didn't know. She seemed willing, going off with that man... that vampire. We didn't know about mind control or vampires... any of it." She cries harder, her lips trembling. "I failed *you*. You died... and I wasn't there. I wasn't there to stop him. I'm so sorry, Claire. I thought I was protecting you by leaving."

I want to reach out to Hailey, to hug her, to comfort her, but if I move, I could disrupt our communication. I wipe my own tears away with the backs of my fingers. The planchette remains still under Hailey's fingers. Is she gone? Had Hailey's words been the peace she'd been seeking? To know that no one thought she'd failed Madison?

"Claire?" I ask. "Are you still there?"

The planchette twitches again, once, twice, before it moves steadily across the board again.

NOT YOUR FAULT.

"She doesn't blame you," I tell Hailey, hoping Claire's words bring her peace now, too. She's been living in guilt, blaming herself for Claire's murder. But as Claire said, it's not her fault. ...It's Sal's fault. Catherine's. They're the ones who'd tormented us all... until we'd finally ended them. Julian killed Sal. Hailey had ended Catherine... on the carousal... after the glass had unexplainably shattered, distracting Catherine and blinding her under splintered shards.

"Wait...," I say. "The carousal."

Hailey wipes more tears away, eyeing me in confusion. "What?"

"The glass. You said it'd just shattered, that you felt a presence."

Her eyes widen as she realizes what I'm saying. She looks at the board again and puts both hands on the planchette once more. "Claire... were you at the fairgrounds that night? Did you... help me?"

The planchette moves directly to *YES*.

I hardly know what to say... and neither does Hailey. Claire was there, in spirit. But how did she manage to shatter the glass on the carousel? I imagine that would take a lot of energy, for a ghost...

The lights suddenly begin to flicker before they finally go out completely. Next go the candles, leaving smoke to float above them in the darkness.

"I thought she wasn't mad," I croak.

In the dark, I see Hailey's frightened eyes looking around the room. I'm sure my expression matches hers: absolutely horrified.

The planchette moves, making us both jump, a gasp erupting from me.

RUN.

I quickly jump up from my chair, sending it falling to the ground behind me with a clash of cheap plastic against cement. My eyes are still on the board, but the planchette hasn't moved. Neither has Hailey.

"She said run," I state, even though I know Hailey read that, too. "Why did she say run?"

Just as the air is chilled, the coolness stickily crawling upon my flesh, the wooden steps leading upstairs begin to creek, as if someone's standing on them. In the dark, I can see plainly that no one is there. At least no one we can *see*.

Hailey stands up just as quickly as I had, her chair screeching across the floor behind her, before she hurls herself around the table to get to me. There in the dark, we hold onto each other as we wait for whatever Claire warned us to run from makes itself known.

If we can't get up the steps, where the hell can we run?

But why should we be afraid? We're both vamps, creatures with sharp fangs, increased strength and speed. For crying out loud, we can escape a spirit or whatever this thing is.

Just as the steps groan louder, the wood seeming to protest under a heavy weight, I rush toward the steps, prepared to run through whatever evil spirit is there.

"Ivy!" Hailey screams behind me.

I want her to see that we're strong, that we can escape whatever malevolent force is here. I don't expect a paralyzing cold to knock the wind out of me, to be unable to breathe as if I'm human again. Now falling onto the steps, I reach up and begin to crawl, to try to escape this chilly force that's sucking the life out of me, one that leaves me feeling the icy cold sting of dread and death deep inside my gut and chest.

"Be gone!" Hailey shouts, a whoosh sounding out as if whatever is here is being sucked out of the room.

I suck in air soon after, my body warming back to its natural cool temperature, one that isn't subzero. For the first time, I feel like I *need* to breathe. After gasping for air for a few seconds, I finally feel like my normal vamp self, like breathing isn't a necessity.

I turn over to see Hailey holding up the black candle and the penis lighter.

"Guess these really are for protection," she says with relief.

"What the hell was that!?" I ask, looking around the room.

Hailey comes toward me, grabbing my hand and lifting me off the steps. "I don't wanna find out. Let's get out of here!"

Chapter 12. Seducing a Wolf

Hailey waits with me until Julian stops by, his arrival announced by the roaring engine of his bike as he pulls along the curb outside Vixen. His presence brings me some peace, but I'm still left feeling unsafe, something I haven't experienced since going to war against the High Society. But instead of rogue vamps with technology on their side, I'm now terrified of a malevolent spirit with psychic powers.

Hailey's been assuring me that the spirit is gone, that she'd sent it back to where it'd come from (closing "the gate", as mentioned in the Ouija board instructions). Maybe it's the fear settled deep in my gut talking, but I don't believe her. I need more black candles to keep lit and on hand, just in case it tries to come back. Velda is about to make another huge sale. I'll grab sage to burn, whatever I need to keep dark forces out of my undead life. I'll chant every day if I have to, whatever words I need to, to keep that thing away from me.

Julian walks into the shop wearing his usual perfectly fitted jeans and a dark grey cotton tee, his brows pulled in with worry for me. He'd felt my fear, my suffocation, when I'd been under attack. He'd called me soon after I'd been in distress, and I'd explained everything while he sped over.

"You sure that thing is gone?" he asks Hailey, just as he pulls me against him and wraps his protective and warm arms around me, cocooning me from the evil of a deadly dimension.

Funny... a vampire fearing evil. I guess even a creature that's feared has fears of their own. Here I am, terrified of something more dangerous than even me. Can Julian protect me from whatever that thing was... if it comes back? Whether he can or not, I'm not certain, but being in his arms provides all the comfort I need. I wrap my own arms around his back to hold him closer to me.

"It's gone," Hailey reassures him. "I closed the gate."

"Closed what gate?" Julian asks.

"I moved the planchette to *Goodbye* before I told it to leave." She pauses. Is Julian looking at her in confusion? Had I not just participated in a séance, all of that would've sounded like a foreign language to me, too. "Look, all that matters is I closed the gate between our dimension and theirs."

Julian breathes in deeply, and I listen to the air filling his lungs in a gentle *whoosh*, the sound of his heart steadily beating inside his chest in a calming tune of *boom boom, boom boom, boom boom*... "All right...," he says slowly, his chest vibrating with his words. He sounds as though he believes all of this is totally strange.

I don't blame him – it *is* strange. I've never dealt with ghosts before, and I don't want to ever again.

Hailey sighs. "Anyway, it's late. I need to see Derick."

"Understood," Julian responds, ending their brief conversation.

I listen as Hailey's boots thud across the carpet leading to the Exit, the smooth grind of a lock being unsecured sounding out next, the door opening and allowing the night air to enter – the sound of the city with its sirens wailing in the distance coming in with the breeze – and her continued walk across the cement of the sidewalk and street toward the garage where she'd parked.

Now we're alone, me and Julian. I imagine the hot pink corset and matching thong hanging off a rack nearby. Hailey had undone the lock, and I'll need to secure it once more to ensure we won't be interrupted. "I should lock up."

"I got it," he says, releasing his hold from me, his hands lingering on my back before they leave coldness behind as he moves away from me.

As he walks toward the door, I take a few steps toward the rack the lingerie is hanging on, reaching out to snag the two items – the corset and thong – before Julian can finish securing the bolt.

When he does turn around, he narrows his gaze upon seeing me with my hands behind my back. "You hidin' somethin'?"

The first time he sees these two pieces, I want them to be on me. "It's a surprise."

The corners of his lips pull up in a slow grin. "A surprise, huh?"

I can't give anything away. The seduction I have in store will be almost agonizingly slow as it plays out. "Mm-hmm."

He begins to thoughtfully walk toward me, each step decided, slow... the predator in him unleashing as the blue green of his eyes brighten. He stops in front of me and leans closer, the warmth of his touch returning as he holds my hips between his hands. That warmth travels as he slides them back across the denim of my jeans, making his way to whatever it is I'm hiding from him.

I've locked eyes with him, my gaze just as heated as his, the vibrant colors of his sea eyes a hue I've become lost in, as though I'm simply a small boat rocking back-and-forth on the waves of stormy waters. It's only me and the sea. Me and Julian. His heart has begun to beat just slightly faster than before, that pounding familiar with the one I feel beginning between my legs.

Before he can touch the lingerie, I back out of his hold with a grin. "Let's go downstairs."

His heart beats even faster now, echoing in my ears, filling the silence.

I nod toward the hall, waiting for him to go ahead of me. Otherwise, he could sneak a peak of what I'm keeping from him.

He grins, letting out a shaky breath, before he heads that way. I keep my body in tune with his, continuing to hide the lingerie behind me. A small chuckle rises from his chest when he sees how secretive I'm being, how intently decided I am on not ruining my surprise for him. I follow behind him as he crosses the shop floor, his thick black biker boots heavy against the carpet. In the hall, he turns the unlocked knob leading to my living quarters, opening the wooden door with a modest squeak. Past the steps and through the living room he goes, before he pauses on the black faux fur rug in the center of the living room.

"Bedroom," I instruct, causing his back to twitch and his heart to pound harder, louder... "Wait for me there."

When he's out of sight, I head for my bathroom and begin to undress, sliding my worn-in light blue jeans away from my hips and legs. I remove the deep crimson Vixen tee showing the icon of an open black lily before shedding my bra and undies. I stare at my reflection for a moment after I've grabbed the thong I'd set down on the counter before.

As I eye myself, I slide the thong on, snapping the strings against my hips once they're in place, gasping from the pleasant sting. On next goes the corset, and I tighten the strings beneath my breasts, swelling them higher. The black stilettos I'd had on add to how sexy I feel. Will Julian be left breathless when he sees me? My top teeth come down against my bottom lip, pulling at it. I watch as I release it, the white from where I'd applied pressure with my teeth turn a light pink again.

I want him to bite me tonight.

After sinking *my* teeth into him last time, it's only fair...

I give myself a wicked smile before I exit the bathroom, my heels clicking against the cement of my living room floor. When I reach the bedroom door, Julian's sitting on the edge of my bed with his hands planted firmly on his knees, waiting for me. I lean against the doorframe, watching his eyes glow brighter than before, hearing his heartbeat quicken much faster, his breathing becoming harder. He's not breathless upon seeing me in my sexy getup as I'd imagined he'd be, but I'm much more partial to the heavier breathing I've inspired from him.

I walk farther into the room before standing in front of him. He's a statue sitting there, unmoving save for his eyes watching my every move, lazily and hungrily taking in the sight of me in a corset and skimpy britches. As I'd fantasized earlier, his eyes move across every inch of me with adoration.

I step between his legs, widening them, before climbing onto his lap and kissing him, my hands at each side of his face, his stubble scratching at my palms. His hands are on my back and thighs as he holds me in place against him, the rough yet soft and warm feel of his skin against mine sending me under into a familiar and consuming haze of passion. With a content sigh into his mouth, I remember precisely what he'd felt like last time: hot, hard yet soft, thick and powerful, unrelenting...

I lean back to look at him, to appreciate him. His astonishing eyes – a vibrant aquamarine – stare back at me just as intensely. "I want you," I whisper, grabbing his jaw – the pricks of his stubble against my fingers rough yet soft – before I possess his mouth with my own once more, wrapping my tongue up with his, the warmth wetness of his mouth heating up the coolness of mine.

Heavier now his breathing has become, as he inhales roughly, then exhales the same – deep and hard. His mouth has claimed mine just as fervently as his fingers have dug into my hips, demandingly pulling me against him. As he hungrily tastes me, his tongue diving deep and twisting with mine, his heart beats louder, faster.

As I rock my hips against his, feeling a thick bulge through his jeans against the thin lace of my underwear, his name comes from my lips, a sigh of a whisper, as he takes me under the same spell he always does. Passion is a heady drug, so intoxicating to the senses that it leaves you wanting more until you've flown as high as you can. Some might even say it's dangerous, leaving you exposed, your guard down, the only thing important in the moment being the need to feel a release from the pent-up desire boiling the blood within your veins, the throb between one's thighs demanding satisfaction.

And it's too much, too overwhelming. I need release.

I slide my hands under his cotton tee, his muscles flexing and twitching beneath my wandering and curious fingers, my palms now warmed as they travel across his heated skin. Needing to feel his bare skin against mine, I pull his shirt upward and over his head, breaking our kiss. He leans into me again after I've tossed his shirt, his stubbled jaw scratching at my neck as he leaves warm, soft kisses against me, the sensation from the two textures making my insides clench and the ache between my legs pound more prominently.

"Julian," I whisper again, his hips twitching beneath mine. "I want you."

He grabs hold of the outside of my thighs, securing me on his lap as he shifts on the mattress, turning us over so he can tower over me. His shadowed features in the darkness of my bedroom, and the growl that rumbles low within his chest as he looks me over, make me tighten my thighs around his waist. If a heart pounded within my chest, it'd have been swelling with love for him, watching him watch me as if I'm the most precious thing in the world. This is *my* wolf, *my* mate...

His gaze wanders to the straps at my shoulders. His hands move across my waist, over my breasts – lingering there as he massages them briefly, provoking a moan to come up my throat and a smile to form across his face hearing the reaction he's inspired from me – before he pulls the straps down, away from my shoulders, down my upper arms, past my elbows and away from my wrists... the top of the chemise coming down as he does, freeing my breasts for his hungered view and admiration.

As he leans down, his warm chest moves closer to them, pressing against them. He tucks my jaw into his palm, urging me to kiss him as his lips collide with mine in a sweet dance – gentle, steady, rhythmic. That same hand that cups my jaw now moves across my neck, straight to the side of my breast pressed so contently against his warm chest. He shifts his weight, leaning to the side so he can touch me, his thumb lightly playing with the bud.

His lips, never leaving mine as he plays, crush against mine harder as I moan inside his mouth. He pushes his hips against mine, his desire for me pressing against the most sensitive part of me. How I burn for this man, this wolf. How have I not caught fire under his touch?

His tongue rubs against mine, his hips doing just the same, his fingers, too...

"Julian," I moan against his lips, begging now. I'd intended to torment him, to make him beg for me to give him release. But here I am, helplessly moaning beneath him, begging him to sate my desire.

His lips stretch and thin against mine now, as he smiles. "I love when you say my name."

Now I smile, and he leans back, his bright irises contrasting vibrantly against his shadowed features.

His fingers work to untie the ribbons holding the chemise together, until the garment has opened up completely, leaving me nearly bare beneath him, save for the underwear.

"Ivy," he hums, his focus moving across my entire frame, his hands – rough yet soft – rubbing up and down the very thighs he's settled between. "I... love more than just the way you say my name." He moves his hands beneath me, taking hold of the tops of the lace underwear, pulling them slowly away from my hips – over my thighs, past my knees he's lifted, and finally away from my ankles. As he watches me, his focus intent on my eyes, he unbuttons his jeans and slides them off, maneuvering his weight on the mattress to do to. His boxers follow next, and both are tossed on the floor before he crawls closer to me, settling himself between my thighs again.

He nuzzles my nose with his, his lips gently pecking at mine. As he stiffens, preparing himself to merge with me, his lips against mine, he says, "I love you. All of you."

With those words, he's pushed himself inside me, and I all but come apart in every possible way. Emotionally I feel elated, his confession mimicking my own feelings for him. Physically I'm satisfied to have the throbbing ache sated, to feel him moving against me, the thick length of him stretching me so wonderfully.

I can't keep the way I feel from him. I moan the words out, my own confession, my own truth: "I love you, too. I've loved you for so long..."

Almost from the moment I saw him, I loved him. I might not have understood it at the time, but those feelings were there, ripe and ready to be explored.

His thrusts against me quicken, his breath hot and urgent against my lips as he moans between kisses.

Soon, we're spiraling, spinning, and the world's falling away just as I reach the edge, just as I let go...

I hold onto Julian, feeling his back muscles rippling beneath my palms, his hips still pushing against me, harder and faster... until he lets go, too.

Now breathless, slick with sweat, heart pounding fiercely in his chest, he plants kisses along my jaw, across my cheeks and on my lips.

I slide a finger across his back, making his hips twitch against me. He nuzzles my neck, sucking on my skin, his tongue flicking and massaging. I sigh, arching my neck and back, pressing my body against his, giving him more space to suck... to bite. "Julian... bite me."

Chapter 13. Bite Me

My words come out a plead, an invitation. They're words he'd once said the same, when he'd willed me to feed from him.

I've wanted Julian to bite me for some time now, ever since he confirmed we're mates. Having been a vampire for countless decades, living an entire lifetime as such a creature, I want something more now. I want a new future, one with Julian... perhaps even children.

Julian's lips leave my neck, but he doesn't move too far away, his breath still hot against the damp part of my neck he'd been playfully tasting. "You... you want me to bite you?"

More than anything. "Yes."

He shifts his weight only slightly, sitting up more to look at me now. He's curious, his brows lower, his eyes narrowed and searching mine for something. "Don't you like bein' a vamp?"

"I want more."

"More of?"

"You." I tighten my legs around his hips. "This."

He chuckles, skimming his fingers along the top of my leg. "Darlin', we can have more of *this* anytime we want."

I reach up and push a dark wave of hair away from his forehead, now searching his eyes. Does he not want more with me? To be wolves together? Stronger mates?

"What is it?" he asks.

"Don't you want more with me?"

"Define more, 'cause I love you just the way you are."

My lips part, a smile forming. "I love you, too. I just..." How can I explain why I want more with him? Why I want our connection to be stronger? It's this gnawing need inside me, really, demanding that I be a wolf. But how can I say that? Doesn't he feel it too, that same ache inside him? A demand to bite me and turn me? "Don't you *want* to bite me?"

"You're askin' me if I wanna hurt you? No, I don't."

"No. I'm asking if you want to turn me, to mold us closer together, to have the chance to be more together."

Now understanding me, his brows lift, and his tense eyes relax. "This is about us bein' mates."

I lightly nod twice, my focus on him intent as I await his response.

"Do you wanna be a wolf?"

I nod again.

"I just didn't think you wanted to be. Figured you're used to this life, the life you've had for eighty-somethin' years."

"I was... until I met you."

"And now you wanna... turn?"

My voice shakes with the thought of this finally happening: "Yes."

"And you want this right now... with me between your legs?"

It's my turn to shift beneath him, my legs loosening a little. "This might not be an ideal position, I agree..."

He chuckles again. "Not exactly, no. Why don't we uh..." He sits up more, moving his hips away from me, the spent length of him sliding out of me, making me moan. "Why don't we get dressed and discuss?"

I guess I thought being bitten after making love would've been romantic, but looking at things from Julian's perspective – being the one to inflict a painful bite on my mate – I can see why he'd want to do this another way. Still, him moving away from me after such an important conversation leaves me feeling rejected. And that's silly, after all, considering how he didn't say no. He just wants to... discuss it further. He could've just said *let's get dressed first*, but he'd instead stated that we should get dressed so we can talk about it.

Wait... we need to *talk* about it? We need to *discuss* it, as he'd said?

I sit up and grab my burgundy satin robe from the antique wooden chair it'd been folded over, quickly wrapping it around my back and sliding my arms through the long sleeves. He's been toying with me long enough. First, he denied me as his mate for reasons that now seem ridiculous to me. Now, he's pulling the same stunt in pulling away from me just as soon as I want us to be fully committed to each other. I tie the sash around my waist brusquely, tightening the bow with a jerk. "If this is something we need to *discuss*, perhaps we shouldn't even consider doing it at all." I turn around to see him pause while pulling his jeans up, the fabric now only around his knees.

"Come again?"

I shrug tensely before waving my hands about. "Why do we need to discuss this, Julian? You either want me to be your mate, or you don't. You either want to turn me, or you don't."

He finishes pulling his jeans up, buttoning them quickly, before he approaches me, standing just a few inches from me, towering over me by nearly an entire foot. "I never said I didn't wanna turn you. I just said let's not do it so soon after..." He gestures to the bed before running that same hand through the dark curls on the top of his head. "Well, you know. Not so soon after makin' love. When I bite you, it ain't just gonna hurt. You're gonna get sick and vomit up any blood you've had recently. You're gonna faint and..." He looks pained. "You'll die first."

My lips part, leaving my mouth hanging open. *Die* first? Madison hadn't mentioned that. "...Wh-what?"

"That's how it happened with Madison and Dorian, and he about damn near lost it. Hell, he *did* lose it! Thought he'd killed his mate, poor bastard. Freaked out for a few minutes before she came to."

I look down at my hands, my fingers twiddling about. "Madison never mentioned that..."

"'Course not. It's not somethin' they like rememberin.'"

I clearly wasn't aware of the entire process. Madison had mentioned getting *deathly* sick, but I didn't realize she'd actually *died*. Now I understand Julian's reaction, and I don't blame him for not wanting to inflict such torment on us both. "So... you... you don't want to bite me, then? Because you don't want us to endure all that?"

His large, warm hands come over my shoulders, covering them, his thumbs rubbing them. "I don't wanna see you suffer."

So, that answers that. Even though being turned now sounds unsavory, I still feel disappointment weighing down my heart. "I understand."

"Ivy... look at me."

I can't look at him.

"Please?" he asks, voice low.

It takes an immense amount of strength for me to tear my eyes away from my fingers, to bring them up to meet his. But I do it. I need to finish this conversation, even though my shaky legs are begging me to run from the room.

"You *are* my mate," he says, urging me with his voice to accept that. "Just because we're not both wolves doesn't make it any less real."

For a moment, I'm confused by his face blurring, but I quickly realize I've begun to cry. Betrayal tears. I wipe them away just as quickly as they've come on, a dampness now on my fingertips. "It's just... I... I have this need inside me, like something's calling out to me, demanding me to take the bite from you. I suppose it's biological. But... I can't change your mind. I won't." I won't ask again. Being rejected this way... it's unbearable. A crushing weight assaults my heart, strangling it violently and painfully.

He inhales deeply, and one of his thumbs wipes at my cheek. "You're angry with me."

"I'm more angry with myself."

"Why?"

"Because I thought..." I shake my head, lowering my eyes again, settling them on the dark spirally curls of his broad and muscled chest. "I thought you'd want this, too." Clearly, I'd been mistaken, believing he'd want all there is to have when you've found your mate.

His voice is now pained: "You thought I'd wanna see you die?"

I raise my eyes, finding his again, seeing pain behind his gaze. "No.... of course not. But knowing I'll come back as a wolf... your wolf... I thought you'd want that."

The pain within his eyes softens as he stares at me. "I want you safe."

I narrow my gaze on him with confidence. "I trust you'll care for me while I'm transitioning, to be there for me when I awaken. I know I'm safe with you."

His shoulders become less stiff, relaxing. But the crease between his brow remains just as deep. "I want us to be closer, too. I just... worry."

I rub his jaw with my thumb, the shadow of his beard caressing me back. "I know. But my suffering will be temporary, and the benefits from turning will far outweigh any pain suffered on my end... and yours."

He looks into each of my eyes several times, his thoughts quiet. What *is* he thinking?

Finally, he speaks: "You really want this, knowin' what has to happen before you change?"

Hope replaces grief in my chest. My lips lift with a small smile. "I do."

A worried look about him still, his chest rises with the deep inward breath he's taken, the air he'd inhaled soon coming out rough from his nostrils. His jaw clenches as he regards me, but it soon relaxes. "Okay... I'll do it."

My stomach summersaults with the realization that things are about to dramatically change for me... for us.

He runs his hand through my hair, lifting it away from my neck. "Where do you want it?" He skims the backs of his fingers over the side of my neck, sending a pleasing tingle through me – beginning where he's touched me, travelling straight to my chest. "Here?"

"Y-yes."

His other hand is at the small of my back, pulling me closer. His head bends down, closing the distance between his mouth and my neck. Soon, I'll have a bite – *his* bite – and our connection will be deeper. I'll be stronger, more able to protect us both.

He lingers when he's closed that distance, his breath coming out hot against my neck, tickling my flesh, leaving me in greater anticipation for the moment when his teeth, sharp and decided, pierce me.

His lips, soft and gentle, leave a kiss there, where his bite will soon be. He nuzzles my neck, inhaling my scent, kissing me again. His tongue, hot and slick, now tangles with those kisses, until the scrape of his canines, just as playfully, glide across the same space.

It begins as a tiny prick, a slow step toward his decision to complete our bond, then a sharper pain when his bite deepens, ending with his mouth closing over the area, his teeth fully sinking into me.

It's just as paralyzing, this pain, as the need to scream and wretch myself away from him is. But this is a choice I've made. It's a choice *we* made. I wanted this, needed this, *craved* this. And the pain, sharp and burning, yet dull and numbing, is not enough to make me regret my decision. My knees give out from the jolting pain, but Julian holds me safely in his arms. He pulls his mouth away from my neck, his teeth leaving behind his mark, my blood on his lips.

Cool blood trickles out of the punctures and slowly slides down my throbbing neck and aching shoulder. Soon, this searing pain will be gone, and I'll be a wolf.

His wolf.

Chapter 14. Missing

I thought it'd be simple, that once a vamp was bitten by their wolf mate, they'd become a wolf. It happened for Madison.

Why not for me?

It's been over twelve hours since Julian bit me. After the mark faded, and the pain was completely gone, I never became ill. I never lost consciousness. A heartbeat never introduced itself inside my chest. My lungs never filled with breaths, nor were they required for me to keep going. And my blood... it still runs just as cool as ever.

I can't help but question my body... and everything that makes me... me. Is there something wrong with me? Am I not chosen to wander the earth as a wolf more strongly connected to my mate and nature?

Now at Vixen, with the light of day streaming in through the glass windows facing the street, I've resumed completing inventory. The basement has been cleaned, with all items that'd been knocked to the ground during Hailey's recent freak-out picked back up and put where they belong. I stare at the display of penis lighters I'd brought up, thinking of my recent tryst with a malevolent spirit. Had my altercation with that spirit somehow altered something within me, leaving me resistant to Julian's bite?

I grab a shiny silver lighter and click it open, a yellow flame coming to life. I watch it continuously burn, the flame reflecting in the darkness of my pupils.

"Ivy?"

I snap my attention away from the flame, finding Hailey standing next to the counter I'm leaning on.

"Everything okay?" she asks, her gaze shifting between me and the lighter.

I snap it closed with a *clink*, extinguishing the flame. "Fine. Why?" I set the lighter back in its rightful place on the small display before

I grab my hot pink pen with the fuzzy end and stare down at the inventory paperwork.

"You didn't even hear me come in."

I tap the fuzzy pink end of the pen a few times against the counter, my focus beginning to drift once again, away from the paperwork to a small scratch on the plastic counter. "I've been distracted, that's all."

"Anything you wanna talk about?"

I look at her again, seeing genuine concern in her eyes and posture – she's toying with the edge of her pinky between the forefinger and thumb of her other hand.

She's a vampire like me, but unlike me, she's found a vampire as a soulmate. Not a wolf, like yours truly. I doubt she'll have any helpful input on my situation, but everything about this situation is eating away at me. I need a friend. I sigh, now resigned to tell her my woes. "It's Julian... or rather, his bite."

She steps closer. "His bite?"

"He bit me last night in an effort to turn me. It was a mutual decision." I snort. "Truthfully, I practically begged for it... but it didn't work on me."

"...Didn't work on you?"

I toss the pen down with a gentle thump against the papers. "I'm still a vamp."

Her brows pull in with confusion. "How is that possible? I thought... I mean... he *is* your mate, right?"

"Of course he is." *...Right?*

"It should've worked."

Her words echo thoughts I've had since last night. While Julian had dozed alongside me in bed, holding me close, believing that at any moment I'd begin to turn, I was awake. I spent the entire night questioning what was wrong with *me*... not *us*. Now I wonder if perhaps we've both been fooled. Julian's words come back to me: *You are my mate. Just because we're not both wolves doesn't make it any less real.*

He'd said that *before* he bit me, before our try at turning me failed. Now that the bite didn't work, is he questioning whether we're truly mates or not? I'd been so sure we were... that we *are*.

"Everyone's different," Hailey sympathizes, coming closer to stand next to me. "I'm sure there's an explanation for this."

"What if we're not mates?" I ask, confessing a fear eating away at me.

She tilts her head and smiles, one of her small hands coming over my shoulder, her large heart-shaped diamond engagement ring Derick had given her glinting in the light. "You are. Don't doubt that."

I can't keep allowing this entire thing to continually upset me. I need a distraction, and now that Hailey's here, getting one is easier. "So, when's the wedding?"

Her lips form a hard line. "You're changing the subject."

"It's better than obsessing over why my body hates me. So... have you saved the date?"

She shrugs and walks off, beginning to fiddle with her ring. "I'm considering next January."

"That's not for a long while. Why not get hitched in a snap in Vegas?"

She laughs, "Because Madison and Dorian already did that."

I wink at her. "Why not make it a tradition among friends?"

She shakes her head, a grin forming, a giggle soon coming out of her. "No! No way! I want a church wedding... I think." Now her brows have become knitted again. "Vamps are allowed in churches, right?"

"I've been in many. Preacher Pete is exceptionally sweet... and a great listener."

"Preacher Pete, huh?"

"Mm-hmm. I've spoken with him dozens of times over the decades."

She opens her mouth to respond, then pauses, her brows creasing even deeper than before. She points a finger at me. "You said decades..."

"I did."

"Does Preacher Pete know you're a...?"

"Preacher Pete knows a lot of things. The man's got weapons in his office. Keeps a crossbow in his pulpit in case there's foul play during a sermon."

"Geez. Has there been before?"

"Back in fifty-two, he said."

"Well, since you know this Pete character so well, would you mind asking him how he feels wedding two undead lovers?" She bats her eyelashes at me, making me laugh.

"Sure thing."

A noise interrupts us, a gentle tapping of sorts on the glass front door. We both look at it, seeing a woman standing outside wearing a dark green cloak, the hood shadowing her features. Her knuckles rap on the glass once more.

"Expecting company?" Hailey asks.

"No..." Who is that? As I look closer, noticing several labradorite rings adorning her pale fingers, I know exactly who this visitor is.

But what would a witch be doing at a vampire-owned establishment? Curious, I walk to the front of the shop and unlock the door, all the while observing her downward glance, as though she's ashamed to have anyone see her here.

I open the door just enough to ask: "Help you with something?"

She edges closer, her voice low: "We need to talk."

"About?"

Head still down, she speaks even lower: "I know what you are... and I need your help."

More curious now, I open the door completely, allowing her to step inside. Once she does, she removes her hood and begins to look around the shop. "Always wondered what it'd be like to stand in here."

"And now that you have?"

She jumps, my presence behind her startling her. "Uh... it's... interesting." She looks at the large assortment of dildos on the wall nearest her. "Very... quaint."

I snort a laugh. "What is it you need help with, Velda?"

She tears her eyes from the large condom selection to regard me now. "It's Mindy, one of my workers. She's gone missing. Never made it home after her shift last night."

"Mindy...," I ponder, remembering the blonde Hailey and I had seen just last night.

"Someone took her," Velda says, her chin lifting in confidence.

"And you know this how?" Hailey asks.

"Let's just say I don't need a Ouija board to contact the dead."

Hailey gives her an intrigued look, but she says no more.

"You're saying spirits told you someone took Mindy?" I ask.

"Not someone... a vampire took her. She's not his first. That's all I know."

Hailey brings her fingers to her lips, her widened hazel eyes on mine, mirroring my horror. "Oh, God..."

Velda turns to look at her. "What is it?" she asks. "You know of him?"

"We've been tracking him," I answer. "He's smart, covers his tracks well. Even wolves can't sniff him out."

Velda's surprised by this, her dark brows lifting, her soft pale pink lips hanging open. "You have werewolves working with you on this?"

I shrug nonchalantly. "Naturally."

"How long have you been searching?"

"Months."

She inhales sharply. "*Months*?!"

"As I said, he's good at covering his tracks." *Too good... alarmingly so.* "If he took Mindy, we'll need to act fast." Though she's probably already dead... I just can't tell Velda something so horrific without having evidence to prove it. All I know is once he takes the girl he's set his eyes on, she doesn't have much time. Hardly any. I walk past Velda, grabbing my knitted black crossbody bag off the back of the chair I'd thrown it on earlier. "Let's go."

Velda looks between Hailey and me. "Where are we going?"

"To see Julian."

"Who's Julian?"

I stop in front of the door, keys I'd fished out of my small bag jingling in my hand. "My werewolf boyfriend."

I turn around, grinning upon seeing Velda's surprise. A vamp dating a wolf? Who would've thought? How scandalous! ...Technically by now I should be a wolf, too. Thinking of that causes my grin to fade fast.

Chapter 15. Witchy Juju

Velda's ditched her emerald cloak, having left it in Hailey's car. Now, she's looking around the police station even more confused than she was when we'd first parked.

"Is your werewolf boyfriend a... cop?" she asks.

I edge closer to her, keeping my voice low: "You'd be surprised how many wolves are. They deal with the supernatural problems the humans are unaware of. And would you mind also keeping your voice down? Not all are in *the know*."

A faint pink brightens her complexion. "Oh. Sorry..."

"This way," I instruct, heading toward several desks with officers seated behind them. I've never actually been to the station before, but Velda and Hailey need not know that detail.

I walk past the desks in my black high-top Converse, noticing several employees eyeing us as we make our way through. One whispers low to another officer: "Dibs on the jean jacket."

He's referring to me, as I'm the one wearing a faded jean jacket over my black Vixen work tee – the waist tied just above the top of my bright red leather skirt that hits mid-thigh. I can't wait to flirt with Julian so he can be disappointed by my unavailability.

"Ladies," the whispering cop bellows, having made his way toward us. "There something I can help you with?"

I turn in time to see him staring at the red leather of my skirt, his focus having been on my backside. "Looking for my boyfriend, actually. Julian Napper..."

As expected, disappointment causes his brows to lower, a faint scowl beginning to appear on his thin, dry lips. "He's around here somewhere. Just saw him not five minutes ago." He turns his attention on Hailey, quickly seeing her engagement ring. When he looks at Velda's hand, seeing too many rings to bother counting, he loses interest fast, turning away.

Hailey looks at me with a grin, and I simply raise a brow while I return the same grin. She'd heard him as well, claiming *the jean jacket* (me) prior to coming over.

"Well that was fun," I mutter, making her grin widen further.

Velda looks between us. "What was fun? What'd I miss?"

I look at the cop who'd just left us, who's now eyeing us again over his computer screen. "Let's just say he was *very* unhappy about me being here for Julian."

She regards him with a quirked brow before her focus strays to the framed pictures on the nearest wall. I don't see Julian's photo, but he's been a cop for "a long time". Probably best not to have photographic evidence of his never-aging appearance available for his fellow officers to behold and question.

Less than a minute later, Julian's thick drawl sounds out: "Ivy?"

I turn to find him wearing his uniform, one that fits him in all the right places. Keys on his matte black belt jingle as he walks our way, and his gun (who really needs one when you've got claws, though?) is secured on that same belt. Beneath the sleeves of his deep navy button-down, his biceps bulge against the hem as though they barely fit inside the shirt. If blood rushed through my veins instead of trickling, a wave of heat would've hit me square in the face, and my heart would've undoubtedly given away my desire if it could beat like normal.

"Julian... can we talk somewhere..." I look around at the several pairs of eyes on us, "in private?" My body might not have given away my desire for him, but the shake in my voice may have.

He looks at Hailey, then Velda (I note his confusion at seeing a stranger with us) before he gestures for us to follow him. We walk past the front desk, the same young woman who'd given us the clear to go back still sitting there, her palm supporting her chin as she blankly stares at her computer screen. Outside, Julian keeps close to me, taking hold of the top of my arm as we walk across the grease-stained lot.

He leans closer to my ear. "Everythin' okay?"

"With me, sure..." *Excluding the fact that I'm not a wolf.* We stop in the middle of the lot. "We have a new development in our vamp serial killer case." I nod toward Velda. "This is Velda."

He squints in the setting sunlight as he looks at Velda, the golden flecks hidden within the blue-green of his irises warming them. "Hey, Velda. You know somethin' 'bout our vamp?"

Velda gets straight to the point: "Mindy, one of my friends... she was taken last night by him. We need to find her."

Julian glances at me, a certain sorrow in his eyes. He knows just as well as I do that Mindy is no more. "Got any leads?"

I shake my head disappointedly. "I hoped you might have something to go on."

His brows knit, the crease between them deepening. "No... nothin' new."

"Can't we go back to the shop and have you sniff around?" Velda asks, stepping closer to Julian.

He looks at me questioningly, and I shrug. "So I let it slip that you're a wolf. She knows I'm a vamp, and I didn't even have to say anything."

Julian sighs before looking toward the station for a moment. "All right, just wait here. I'll be back." He nods at me reassuringly before he walks off.

I turn my focus on Hailey and Velda, the two of them anxiously twiddling with their own fingers, unaware that the other is doing the same exact thing.

I want to give Velda reassurance, to say something like *We'll find her* or *Everything will be all right.* But I can't say either of those things. The chances of Mindy being alive are terribly slim. And the odds of Julian being able to track this vamp now when we've been unsuccessful in our hunt this entire time is even lower.

When Julian returns, he's not alone. With him is a wolf not dressed in a uniform but rather faded jeans and a white and grey baseball tee-shirt. I recognize that bronze complexion and sparkling peridot eyes cautiously regarding me: Landon.

I step in front of Hailey and Velda, shielding them. "What's the meaning of this?" I demand of Julian.

"He's with us," Julian explains.

They're still walking toward us, and when they get closer, I bare my fangs and hiss at Landon. "That's far enough!"

Landon abruptly stops, his shoulders stiff as he eyes my fangs.

I look at Julian next. "The hell you mean he's with us?!"

"He came to me lookin' for a pack. Left his own. I was talkin' with him when I heard you were here lookin' for me, too."

I look at Landon again, seeing red remembering his involvement with Denise, how he'd strangled me before losing his resolve. "And we're in the business of taking in untrustworthy strays now, are we? He attacked me at the barn!"

"That was a mistake," Landon admits. "I let you live, didn't I?"

I scoff, "*Let* me live?! Sure, after you choked me!"

Landon shifts his muddied Converse-clad feet, glancing at Julian before he eyes me again. "I thought I was protecting someone worth it. We've all been betrayed by Denise."

I simply seethe, now at a loss for words. I can't trust Landon, even if he had *let* me live, as he so eloquently put it. Julian's usually just as cautious as I am. Is it Landon's species that makes trusting him easier, or is it perhaps a male thing? Denise screwed Julian over, then Landon. Does that mean they've somehow bonded over a mutual screwing-over?

Julian, sensing my unease, begins to further explain things: "His best friend Maverick slept with Denise behind his back. Even though this Maverick guy betrayed his pack by shackin' up with someone else's chosen partner, they refused to turn him out. So... Landon left instead. He sought me out and asked if we're lookin' to expand our pack."

Maybe pity is the cause for Julian's lapse in judgement. Still watching Landon, I ask Julian: "And does Landon here know our pack isn't *just* wolves?"

"I'm aware," Landon answers, his posture now taller. "I care more about loyalty from those in a pack I'm part of, not their race."

I narrow my gaze, still untrusting of him. But we don't have time at the moment to stand around discussing Landon's interest in our pack or my disdain on the matter. So, I grit my teeth and mutter, "Fine," putting an end to this conversation... for now.

Velda steps around from behind me. "Now that that's settled, can we go? We're losing time."

Landon's eyes brighten when he catches sight of Velda, the green of his irises glowing fiercely as his gaze travels from the top of her head, over her voluptuous hips, and right down to her black boots. Out of all the beating hearts around us, one becomes louder, faster, pounding dramatically... Landon's. Having turned around to walk off after giving her two cents, Velda hadn't seen this reaction from him. I'm all for people moving on romantically, especially after being betrayed as Landon had been... but his obvious attraction toward Velda puts me on guard. She might not be my friend (more of an ally), but I don't trust this wolf. He better keep his paws off her.

I follow her and Hailey toward Hailey's car.

Julian's begun to walk just as the rest of us have, but he grabs my hand at one point and gently pulls me along with him. "We'll follow 'em. Ain't no room in that little car Hailey drives."

I sputter my disapproval: "Y-you're leaving them alone with Landon?!" I ask, looking at the backs of the three of them as they retreat toward Hailey's car. Landon's keeping his distance behind Velda.

"They'll be fine."

I scowl at him. "You have an awful lot of faith in a wolf who *dated* Denise!"

He grabs my pink helmet and places it over my head. "You forget I let her be part of my pack for *years*. You know, before I really knew she was the deceitful type. He deserves a second chance."

Still, I scowl.

He sighs, "If he fucks up, I'll rip his head off. Sound fair?"

While he secures my chin strap, I glare at him. "Before or after he hurts our friends?"

"Velda's a friend now, huh?"

My glare deepens. "You're missing the point, Napper."

He chuckles. "Yeah, I got your point… Panagakos." He grabs each side of my helmet and leans down to look at me straight-on. "Look, he ain't gonna do nothin', all right? He's got a broken heart, is all. Denise really did a number on him."

I keep glaring silently.

"Look… I know you don't trust him, but you trust me, right?"

Begrudgingly, as I know where this is going, I nod.

"Then trust me when I say he ain't gonna hurt no one."

My glare softens, turning to worry. "Not even you? You're the wolf who…" I don't want to say *killed*, but… "… killed his girlfriend."

His hands drop from my helmet, moving to his front pant pockets instead. He watches me silently for a moment, his brow creasing with seriousness. "We talked about that."

"You did?"

He nods.

"And?"

His feet shift, his shoulders tensing. "He knows I did it to protect my mate. She would've killed you."

"But didn't he love her like you love me?"

He shrugs, shoulders still tense. "He said that love began to fade when he found out about her affair with his best friend. It vanished for good when he found out what she did to me and my pack. He finally saw her for who she really was – someone who didn't care about anyone but herself. Not even him."

Still, I regard him with worry.

His eyes are set in determination as he stares back at me. "He won't hurt you or me or anyone else. I won't let him."

I could stand here and argue with him some more, but Hailey's already started her car, the engine roaring to life in the distance. We can discuss this later, I suppose. Right now, we need to look for Mindy. So, I quietly mutter: "Fine."

"He could've killed you at that barn," he points out. "He didn't. He even stood his ground and was prepared to protect you when Denise was gonna do it. Remember?"

Right, he'd *let* me live. "...Yeah, I remember."

"All right, then. I'm gonna be straight with you. I don't know many wolves that would've defended a vamp they didn't even know against a wolf they'd partnered up with."

Julian's right, I suppose. Landon stood up against Denise when she was prepared to rip me to shreds at that barn. Wolves don't usually choose a bloodsucking stranger over another wolf, regardless of the circumstances. "Fair enough," I sigh, looking back again to see Hailey backing out of the space she'd parked in. "We better start following them."

He winks at me before kissing me and closing my shield. He gets on his bike first, and I settle myself behind him. He squeezes my hand where it rests against his abdomen before he starts his bike, the engine roaring loudly. He kicks the stand up, grips the handles and revs the engine before speeding off to follow the others. I snuggle up against his back, squeezing the outside of his thighs against the inside of mine like I always do, my leather skirt riding up as I straddle him.

At Wix, Julian and Landon use their tracking skills – including their heightened sense of smell – to determine where Mindy may have gone. Hailey and I look for clues the killer vamp might've left behind, travelling past the shops surrounding Wix in the strip and all the way past Vudu over a block away. As I carefully do my best to look for signs of Mindy's abduction, I find nothing indicating she was taken forcefully (no blood, damaged property, lost shoe, etc.). This vamp enjoys mind controlling his victims to helplessly and silently follow him toward their own death. I doubt we'll find anything indicating a struggle.

When I return to Wix, meeting up with the others, everyone's empty-handed and clueless.

While the others speak with each other, I study Julian, his curious eyes taking in Wix for the first time, his gaze settling on transparent jars of herbs on one of the many wooden shelves. He picks one up and examines its dried-up, green contents. "The hell is this for?"

I lean closer, whispering: "Keeps goblins away from one's yard. They piss all over the place... it's why you see that yellow grass sometimes... totally destroys the blades."

Even more taken aback now, he looks between me and the jar with alarmed eyes. "You serious?"

I snicker. "No!"

He glares at me for a moment before putting the jar back on the shelf. "You're always screwin' with me."

I smile up at him as warmly as I can. "You make it easy, my love."

Velda, frustrated by our lack of clues, grabs a candle from where she's been pacing, one she'd lit while asking the spirits for guidance, and throws it across the shop, the glass shattering and white wax spattering a black wall and dotting anything within a ten-foot radius. Glass skitters across the floor in busted shards, some pieces landing near my shoes.

Landon watches her worriedly. "We'll find her," he assures her.

My heart sinks knowing his words aren't necessarily true. None of the missing girls' bodies have been recovered. Even if we do find Mindy, she won't be alive, will she?

Mimicking my thoughts, Velda's shoulders slump, her eyes on the black, white-wax-spotted floor as she says, "You don't know that."

"Anythin' else we can try?" Julian asks.

She inhales carefully, expelling it shakily. "One other thing. It's a last resort. I wanted to try other options first, but we're now out of those. The spirits don't want to mess with the balance of things, so they're refusing to tell me where she is." She looks at the ceiling angrily. "Why they even bothered telling me she was taken by a vampire is beyond me!"

Her increasing heartrate pounds anxiously within her chest. I step closer to her. "What is it, this last resort?"

She looks between us all, taking another deep breath. "Inducing visions."

"Inducing visions?" Landon asks. "What does that mean?"

"It means," Velda says, moving past us and heading toward the back of the shop, her boots clicking against the starry black tiles, "I have to go under, sort of like falling asleep, in order to be shown what I need to see. It takes a lot out of me, and it disrupts the balance in the universe. As such, I've only done it once before."

I follow her. "This whole disruption of the universe deal... the balance being off... what exactly does that mean?"

She leads us into a large room at the back of the shop. The walls are black, as are the tiles (like the rest of the shop). Only a small green lamp sitting on a chipped-up wooden desk in a corner lights up a portion of the room. There are no windows here, so no natural light filters in (though it'll be dark soon, anyway). Wooden shelves stained dark and nearly tall enough to reach the ceiling sit against one wall, each shelf lined with filled glass jars and books secured in tattered leather covers. A black pleather futon sits at the end of the room, a plum-colored faux fur blanket and a matching oversized pillow covering half of it. Another modest shelf of books sits near the futon, the contents appearing to be books for pleasure reading, not studying the dark arts like the leatherbound ones are likely used for. Clothing hangs from velvet black hangers on a clothes rack with wheels.

Does she sleep back here? ...Does she *live* here?

Velda lights a black candle housed within a large glass jar, her features brightening. "There are always consequences to using magick as I do. It's borrowed magick... it doesn't always come from within me. I take it from the universe. And... I have to pay the price."

"Which is?" I ask.

"Some spells leave me weakened and exhausted for days, my energy absorbed. My connection to the spirits might be stripped. Others, like this one, requires blood." She looks at me for a moment, then Hailey, who's taken to standing next to me. "You might want to leave if you can't handle that part."

Ye of little faith. I give a confident response: "We can handle it."

Velda nods before grabbing a mason jar containing bits of green herbs, the metal lid grinding against the glass as she opens it. She pours some of the herbs into a small matte black ceramic dish before grabbing a box of matches and swiping the red end across the box, igniting the tip a blazing yellow. She tosses the match into the bowl, setting the herbs afire, the white smoke rising and filling the air with a pungent stench. Julian coughs before waving his hand in front of him to dispel the smoke in the air. Being sensitive to smells, more so than a vamp, his senses are likely overwhelmed by the awful bitter smell.

Velda retrieves a sterling blade with a Celtic design on the handle, using the tip to prick her finger, a wince emerging from her (and

Landon twitching next to her) before she allows the few drops to fall into the bowl of burning herbs. She sets the knife down and grabs a tissue to hold against her finger before she crosses the room, settling on the futon, resting her back and head on the purple pillow. Now closing her eyes, she inhales deeply before reciting unintelligible words.

The candle she'd lit and set down begins to flicker before it goes out entirely, reminding me of the séance Hailey and I had performed. As such, I step closer to Julian, firmly grabbing hold of his beefy arm. Hailey steps closer to us as well, her eyes widened more than usual as she watches Velda. She grabs hold of my arm, holding onto me just as I am holding onto Julian.

Motionless and breathing deeper, Velda appears asleep. Her spell must be working, then. Her eyes move beneath her lids, back-and-forth as though she's in the REM stage of sleep. She must be experiencing those visions she'd intended to have.

What must she be seeing wherever she is?

Chapter 16. Juniper Bayou

We waited as Velda was under, trapped beneath the spell she'd created to help us find her friend. I'd noticed at one point that Landon's stare was rather direct on Velda, his focus unmoving from where she laid on the futon. It was like she was the only thing that existed in his world, his thoughts unspoken as the rest of us exchanged whispered curiosities about how long she'd be under, what those herbs were and what happened the last time she did this (she'd said she did it only once before).

Now, not fifteen minutes after she'd closed her eyes and her breaths had become deep with sleep, she's awakened, darkened blue eyes settling on Landon for a moment before she blinks herself out of his transfixed stare. Rising from the futon, she rubs at her left temple with her uninjured hand.

"Well?" I ask, impatient now to know the details of her visions.

Brows pulled in as far as they can be, a severe line between her eyes, her gaze is haunted as she stares at the black tiles. A tortured whisper leaves her lips: "...Juniper Bayou."

A location. That's definitely a start. But Velda doesn't look hopeful like one would expect. "What else did you see?"

She clenches the bloodied tissue she'd used to stop the bleeding from where she'd pricked herself. "I was in the water. ...I was grabbed and dragged down. My ankles were bound together by something pulling me under. I think... I think he's keeping their bodies in the bayou."

I swallow back the lump in my throat. Have the vampire's victims been submerged within the murky waters of the bayou like she suspects? "*Their* bodies?"

Velda nods, her eyes now regarding the floor with utter despair.

Julian takes a step forward. "I know Juniper Bayou. It's in Shawhill County, at least an hour from here."

If there's a chance Mindy's alive, we need to get on the road now. I nod at Julian. "Let's go."

He agrees with a nod of his own before he glances at Landon. "Stay with Velda. Keep her safe."

Velda stands from the futon, determination in her stance and gaze as she looks at Julian. "I'm going, too."

Julian's tone is serious, authoritative: "No, you're not."

But Velda isn't dissuaded by his tone, even if it warns one not to argue with him. She stands her ground. "I refuse to sit here and wait."

Julian shakes his head, silent now, likely debating on whether arguing with her will do any good.

"We're wasting time," Velda admonishes, walking forward, straight for the door to leave the room. "Let's go."

I've never been to Juniper Bayou, but like the name suggests, the air is filled with the scent of cedar and fruit, a sweet yet citrusy combination from the overgrown Juniper trees and shrubs nearby. The scent is overpowering, leaving my head uncomfortably filled with it. Stabbing it, really. Vampires don't get headaches, but the memory of them from my life as a human remains intact, bringing awareness of what's going on as a spark of a pain teases at my temples. Cicadas rattle on in the distance, hiding away as they sing their songs much too loudly, their tune piercing my eardrum like a buzzing knife.

Surrounding the bayou is a rusted metal fence, the color of it completely orange, the last of its paint worn away with age. Overgrown grass and weeds line the sidewalk on the edge of the bayou, their green ends tickling the cement as they sway with the breeze. And the water – murky as I'd imagined it, reminding me of a shadowed pit where all things are taken and lost forever – moves with gentle waves as the same breeze blows past it. The sky has darkened an eerie greenish-grey with the emergence of a storm, thickening the air, foretelling of dreadful things to come.

And then there's the dock made up of wood just as unkept as the metal fence, rotted and stained an unpleasant brownish-green as it stands over the vast space of water stretching out before it. Velda takes the first step onto the dock, looking out over the blackened water as her emerald cloak whips out behind her from a fiercer wind, the wood complaining beneath her boots.

Landon puts a hand on her shoulder. "One of us should go. This thing could collapse."

Eyes still on the water, Velda barely whispers: "It's stronger than it suggests."

She takes another step, but this time, Julian places one of his larger hands on her other shoulder. "We don't know exactly what's out there. Stay here. Let me go."

Velda debates this for a moment before she finally takes a step back, allowing Julian to proceed. The rest of us stay back, waiting for Julian to confirm how sturdy the dock is or if he's found something as he searches between the boards beneath his muddied boots. Halfway up the dock, the wood lets out a lengthy groan before splintering deafeningly, the dock collapsing and Julian falling straight through and into the water with an unsettling splash. As I've run up the dock, he's come up for air, sputtering the dank water out of his mouth and wiping at his eyes. When he sees me leaning over where the wood had given out, sighing in relief upon seeing he's okay, he holds his hand up for me to stay put.

"Don't come down here," he instructs. "Gonna have a look down below while I'm in here."

I nod, just before he dives into the water, his boots the last thing I see as the bayou takes him.

"Aren't there alligators in bayous?" Hailey asks from where she stands beyond the rotted wood.

Landon snorts. "We're werewolves."

"So you're saying...?" she hedges.

"I'm saying even predators shy away from us. But even if they didn't, we can take 'em."

Why do I feel like his eyes are on me? Is it because wolves consider vamps predators? Our serial killer vamp certainly is.

Little bubbles come up after Julian's descended into darkness. I watch them silently, my fingers gripping the edge of the jagged board where Julian had fallen through. When larger air pockets come to the surface, bubbling and creating foam, I nearly jump in after him, but through the dark water, his figure comes to the surface. Had there been a need to breathe, I'd have been holding my breath until he'd come back. When his saturated dark hair finally shows above the water line, curls no longer intact from being weighed-down, shiny strands stuck to his face, he moves those damp ends away from his eyes, looking up at me. A flash of light sizzles above us, lighting up his eyes and reflecting off the glittering water, just as thunder rumbles, shaking the boards beneath me. A needle-like pain digs into my temples, penetrating deeper and deeper into my skull. He grips one of the pillars, steadying himself in the water, as though something is weighing him down, pulling him down. His face is morphed as though he's in pain: lips slack, damp brows curved down dramatically over his worried grey eyes.

"What happened?" I demand, reaching for him, offering a hand. "An alligator?"

He doesn't take my hand. "No... I... I found them."

Hailey shouts in the distance: "Everything okay?"

I barely speak my next words to Julian, my voice low and shaky, unrecognizable as it's tainted with grief: "*Them*?"

He breaths out deeply, expelling a pained sigh that matches the rest of his features. "All of them." He shakes his head, lowering his gaze away from mine, his voice, too. "He tied cement blocks to their ankles to keep 'em down."

"And Mindy?" I whisper, not wanting Velda's human ears to overhear. "Please tell me Mindy isn't down there, too."

But Julian nods, confirming my fear, just before he lifts something up from the water, bringing it to the surface with him.

Something I've hardly ever felt in all my time as a vampire washes over me. My un-beating heart struggles as a clenched fist seems to hold it captive. My stomach churns so profoundly that its contents swirl straight up my esophagus. As I stare at Mindy's face – which is nearly colorless if not for the greenish tint to her paled flesh and the tangled, wet strands of her blonde hair partially strewn across her forehead, her throat ravaged yet unbloodied from where the vampire had feasted on her like a rabid animal – anything that'd been kept down comes rushing out of me, expelling blood I'd fed on earlier all over the dock beneath my trembling hands and weakened knees, coating the mossy wood a stunning red. I wretch and wretch, my body demanding I release all that's been consumed, even when there's nothing left. When the red swims, turning a rusted brown as it merges with the dingy green, blackness playing at the edges of my vision as my head begins to throb with a stabbing pain that now demands my full attention, I can't hold myself up any longer.

Chapter 17. The Turning

A voice is distant, panicked, becoming louder and clearer as I swim up for air, gasping for it as soon as I reach the surface, the darkness that'd kept me under now letting in some light. Warmth surrounds me, securing me in an unforgiving embrace, my hips straddling theirs.

Julian.

His heart beats strong against my chest, pounding out a frantic tune that coincides with each quickened breath. His voice, low and deep and heavy with worry, rumbles from within that chest as he speaks my name: "Ivy..."

I remember vividly how my head had pounded as though blood rushed through it while on the dock at Juniper Bayou, the pain I'd felt unusual yet distantly familiar from when I'd had the occasional headache as a human.

"I must've fainted," I declare, waiting for the pain to return as the intrusive thought of Mindy's corpse appears at the forefront of my thoughts. I'd expected she was dead, but I'd still had hope she wasn't. "It's been such a stressful week, I suppose." His heated arms still hold me captive, refusing to release me, though I don't dare complain. This is where I'm safest, where I'm home. Despite this comfort I now have, I know of a certain witch who must be incredibly grief-stricken and inconsolable, my own heart aching with what I know she must be feeling. "How's Velda holding up?"

Julian's long fingers, heated and gentle, caress my back. "She went with Landon and Hailey after you..." He sighs, somehow managing to hold me tighter.

"After I what? After I fainted?"

I wait until his silence finally startles me, opening my eyes to look over his shoulder, seeing we're alone in a room. Someone's bedroom. A plain oak dresser worn with scratches and dents that show its mature age sits against a wall, the only thing standing atop it a simple cream-colored lamp with a matching shade that lights up an otherwise dark room. The curtains to the left of us are beige, colorless like the rest of the room, whose walls are painted white. Through the fabric, which is nearly transparent, no light comes through, though a relentless tapping on the glass can be heard as the storm that'd come through continues to bring an angry rain. The mattress beneath us is covered with a cotton comforter just as colorless as the rest of the room. Oatmeal, I think the color.

"Where are we?" I ask.

"My place. It was closer."

I've been to his place before... just not his bedroom. There were several nights when we went over notes and evidence on Denise and the serial killer vamp. We'd spent our time in his dining room, sitting at a small, nicked-up wooden table discussing everything. His place is certainly closer to Juniper Bayou, nestled perfectly between Whispering Creek and Blumhaven. "I must've startled you with passing out. Sorry about that." He remains quiet. He's worried. "I assure you that's atypical for us vamps. I won't go fainting on you again any time soon."

He sighs again, the sound speaking of a weight within his own chest. "Ivy... you... you're... different."

Now I'm alarmed, hearing how strained his voice has become, the intense beating of his heart seeming to pound straight into mine. "Different?"

He holds me tighter. "Don't you feel it?"

I take a moment to assess myself, to feel anything other than Julian's warmth and his chaotic heart beating much louder, much...

I pause my thoughts, listening intently now, focusing on the throbbing, gushing, beating... *second* heart. I inhale a stunned breath, realizing now that I've been taking in air and expelling it just the same. I'm *breathing*. It's second nature, and I hadn't even noticed I'd been doing it till now.

"Am I..." But I can't ask it, not when the answer could be cruel, skewering any hope I may have.

His stubbled jaw tickles at the top of my scalp. "You turned."

My fingers dig into the back of his shirt where they're holding him against me, my nails assaulting the soft fabric. *I'm a...?* I can't even think the word, even though I've been clinging to the idea of becoming something different, of being Julian's mate in every possible way, of feeling like that part of me that's been missing has finally been filled. Has that moment arrived? *Am I... a...?*

"Madison was young," he continues, "barely turned when Dorian bit her. But you were a vamp much longer than her, and it took longer, I guess... for the bite to work."

Everything in the room swirls, blending and blurring beneath the burning moisture in my eyes, my voice barely a whisper as tears that normally feel cool tumble over my bottom lids, falling down my cheeks hot: "Is this real? Am I not dreaming?"

"It's real."

I'd begun to feel unwell as soon as we'd reached the bayou, the scent of juniper overwhelming, the cicadas buzzing much too loud. After seeing Mindy, I'd become nauseated, soon vomiting blood. Between the dock and Julian's, I'd turned. "Everything went black... at Juniper Bayou."

"You..." His fingers at my back gather a fist-full of my shirt tightly in his hands. "You died." His voice cracks on the last word. "I panicked. Tried to resuscitate you on the dock. Nothin' worked. Hailey drove us here and called Dorian on the way. She kept sayin' you had to be okay, that you'd come back. Dorian said so, too. I wanted to believe them, but I was so frantic. I thought I'd lost you. I've never been so terrified of anythin' before. I just kept holdin' you, waitin'... for such a long time... until I started to lose my mind thinkin' you were really gone. I'd never have forgiven myself if you were."

I raise my face toward his, my nose skimming his collarbone before he loosens his hold on me so I can look at him. His eyes are nearly lost beneath the pooling tears, the whites of them entirely pink, making the blue-green of his irises stand out much brighter, much greener. I raise one of my hands so I can wipe at the rivers running over his stubbled cheeks down to his chin, so I can try to smooth out the deep line etched between his thick brows. His pain is my pain, emanating from within him straight into me, constricting my own now beating heart. "I'm here, Julian."

He closes his eyes, brows still furrowed so deeply, pressing his forehead to mine, releasing his hold on me just enough to slide one of his hands up to my face, holding it against his palm. "I love you so much."

A tremble begins to play on my lips, my breath hitching hearing how broken he'd sounded. "I love you too, Julian. I'm not going anywhere." The sides of my quivering lips begin to turn up. "You're stuck with me, you know."

A breath of a laugh escapes him, his warm lips finding mine. They're both soft yet hard against mine, gentle yet desperate, the love we feel seeming to swirl around us like an electrified and magical energy, leaving us the only two in existence. The world, as it often does with him, falls away.

His teeth pull at my bottom lip, tugging it softly, his lengthened stubble delectably scratching against my jaw and neck as he moves his mouth across my own now overheated skin. Quickened, pounding heartbeats sound out from the both of us, a sweet and alluring song. And my pulse, as such, throbs in my ears, under my skin, exposing me to sensitivities I'd yet to feel before: My skin now burns much hotter, the blood rushing through my veins like molten lava. Each delectable kiss he plants along my impassioned and hyperaware flesh leaves me sweltering and aching for more.

Still straddling his hips, I push myself against him, holding his face between my hands, deepening the kiss, biting down on his bottom lip just hard enough to cause both pleasure and pain, wrenching a moan from him just before my tongue collides with his once more. Julian's hips twitch beneath me as I gyrate mine, all the while tugging on the wavy hair at his scalp and memorizing the prickly stubble of his beard as my fingers run along it.

I'm much too hot, my clothing an unbearable shield separating us. As he spreads kisses along my neck, his tongue gliding over my flesh as though he's hungry for me, I lose myself in him. I want to fall apart beneath him. I crave it so deeply, my body responds of its own will, my back arching and hips quickening their pace as they gyrate against him.

One of his hands grabs at my hip, lifting my skirt so his heated palm runs along my thigh, burning me up all the more. Desperate now, I moan, "I want you, Julian."

He grabs at my underwear, pulling them away from my hips as he leans up and lies me down, my back pressing into the soft comforter, both his hands now at my hips, pulling the fabric down my legs, tossing the garment away. He joins me once again, his hips between my legs as I cling to him, his mouth hot on mine once more. I pull at his shirt, lifting it, disposing of it after that brief moment our lips parted so he could remove it entirely. His hips push against me, and I reach between us, unbuttoning his jeans, aching for our skin to touch, for him to satisfy me and replace this throbbing ache with a most astonishing release.

I slide his zipper down, reaching inside to grab hold of his shaft, moaning in delight upon feeling how rock-hard he's become, the tip of him moist with his own desire. He groans into my mouth, shimmying out of his slacks and briefs, my hold on him broken as he breathlessly and quickly removes the last of his clothing separating us. He then leans down again, unzipping my leather skirt. My hips lift as the fabric is pulled away from them and down my legs, soon tossed alongside the rest of our clothing on the floor.

Julian's between my legs now, his mouth hungrily over mine, his hands running all over me as though he can't get enough, as if every kiss is our first and every touch too. As if the kisses I return and every touch I give back gives him life. The hard length of him pushes against my inner thigh, until I move my hips, tightening my legs around his hips, yearning for him to fill me. As he does, the entire blissful length of him stretching me and sating that throbbing ache as he pushes deeper, until he cannot go any farther, rips satisfactory moans from us.

I've been waiting my entire life for this, to feel this connection, to feel *him*.

This time is different. This time is everything. This time we're equals.

Julian breathes hard against my lips, my own breath mingling with his, heating us more, as his hips move with purpose against mine, each thrust bringing me closer to reaching that release I've been yearning for.

And when I do, my back arching and hips pushing against his, matching his movements, crying out his name, he follows, releasing into me, sighing my name as the last of his orgasm fades, leaving us breathless and sated... for now.

Chapter 18. Learning to Howl

Darkness has fallen over us, as the sun has set and the storm has continued on, a constant pattering and distant, echoing boom reminding us of what's occurring in the world outside of the one we've tumbled into quite happily.

Satisfied in every possible way, addicted entirely to what this wolf makes me feel – warm, loved, sated – I'm left utterly spent in his arms, nearly dozing as he already has under the lulling power of distant thunder. Even the crickets and frogs have come out to play, holding what I imagine to be conversations among each other, their voices rising over the tapping of rain as each drop collides against the shingles just above us, on the glass just next to us. It's all music, a beautiful melody. This world is calm, peaceful. Nothing can ruin it. At least, I try not to let anything ruin it. I push away the intrusive thoughts threatening to emerge from the shadows of my mind, reminders of today's haunting discovery scratching like claws against my memory, begging me to face it all.

Eventually, though, it becomes difficult to stay locked away in such bliss when Julian's cell, which sits somewhere on the floor, rings incessantly for several minutes.

Julian's prickly beard scratches most delightfully against my neck as he breathes in my scent and snuggles closer, his arms pulling me tighter against him, a satisfied *hmmm* emanating from his throat.

"Have you slept at all?" he asks against my neck, his voice rugged yet soft, his breath warm against my sensitive skin under his lips, the tickling sensation sending shivers of excitement through me.

My lips spread out, a smile forming. "No. I was too busy reveling in the bliss of us."

He chuckles, kissing my neck, the stubble on his jaw tickling me more.

His ringtone sounds off again, the standard tune interrupting us. "It must be an emergency," I say. "I'm surprised you slept through it as long as you did. It's been ringing for at least ten minutes."

He kisses my neck one last time before leaving my side, a chill hitting my backside when he's left the bed. He bends over in his nude glory, picking up his navy slacks and fishing for the phone within the pockets. The phone had stopped ringing, but it resumes once more just as he's found it.

He puts the cell to his ear. "What's up?"

My ears perk up hearing the voice on the other end. Hailey: "Is she...?"

Julian looks at me. "She's okay."

A sigh of relief escapes her. "And?"

"She turned."

Silence now.

Is Hailey still with Velda? "How's Velda?" I ask.

Julian repeats the question to Hailey.

"That's the other reason I've been calling. She flipped when we got back to her shop. Started rushing around the shop gathering things. ...She did a spell, Julian."

His brows pull in with concern, his gaze falling to the carpet, dread in his tone: "What kind of spell?"

Chills spread across my frame, and I sit up fully in bed, watching him, waiting for Hailey's response.

"The bad kind," Hailey answers. "It was scary as hell. She wanted to find the vamp. She was in a frenzy, angry... broken over Mindy's death. She's tracking him now."

"You with her?"

"Not exactly..."

"Not *exactly*?"

"Well... we tried to stop her, me and Landon. That didn't bode well for either of us. I just woke up on the floor. Landon's still unconscious.

I need someone who can actually *track*... I need a wolf. And the one I got ain't exactly helpful since he's knocked out."

Julian looks at me again. "We'll be there. Give us a few." He hangs up and pulls a pair of jeans out of his closet. "You ready to learn how the wolves do things?"

My heartbeat quickens, excitement travelling through my veins. "Absolutely."

At Velda's shop, Landon's lying on his back on the black tile, his eyes closed... knocked out cold just like Hailey said.

Hailey paces, her arms folded across her chest tightly. "She's gonna get herself killed," she panics.

I turn to Julian. "How can we track her?"

He grabs Velda's green cloak, the one tossed on top the cash register counter. He brings it to his nostrils, breathing in the scent. "We can sniff her out," he says, looking out the window just as lightning streaks across the sky. "But with the rain, it'll be difficult." He sets the cloak down, placing his hands on his hips as he looks up at the sky from the window.

"Is there another way?"

"Listen to your gut. Trust it." He shrugs. "Ask for help."

"Help?"

He turns to face me, grinning wickedly. "Ever howled at the moon before?"

I laugh, "Not exactly."

He winks at me. "Time to learn, darlin'."

Damn, he's hot.

Hailey stops pacing. "I don't suppose I can help with that."

Julian regards her with a smirk. "By howlin'? No. But your skills as a vamp will come in handy, especially since we're dealin' with one. You're quick like him. You can help chase him down if need be."

I take a step forward. "Let's get started, then. Time isn't exactly on our side."

Julian grabs Velda's cloak again. "We still might be able to catch her scent." He hands it to me. "Take a whiff, memorize it."

I take the cloak from him and bring it to my nose, inhaling deeply, taking in the mix of smells: lavender, burning sage, laundry detergent, musk...

"Got it?" he asks me.

I smile at him. "Got it."

He glances at Landon's unconscious figure. "Guess we're gonna have to leave him behind."

"He'll wake up in a panic," I worry aloud, knowing of his crush (or quite possibly deeper wolf-mate attachment) to Velda. "We should leave a note at least."

Julian looks around, grabbing a black leather notebook from a shelf, a perfectly new journal with crisp, unmarked pages and a candle symbol on the front, one that matches the shop's icon. He rips a page from it, grabs a pen from a jar containing several of them (all with tall feathers on their ends – the one he grabs is violet) and begins scribbling a message on the paper, folding it in half and setting it on Landon's chest straight after.

"All right, let's go," he says, heading for the door.

I put Velda's cloak back on the counter, giving Landon one final look before I leave.

"Where to?" I ask, hurriedly following behind him with Hailey up the puddled sidewalk, passing up the strand of shops, the three of us becoming doused as the rain and wind picks up.

He sniffs the air, turning a corner soon after. "You smell that?" he asks me. "Her perfume, her skin."

I inhale deeply, urging all the other scents mixing together away so I can focus on the lavender, the sage... the... copper? I pause. "Is that... blood?"

"Yeah," Julian confirms.

"It's mine," Hailey says. "She must've taken it while I was unconscious. I remember her telling me she needed my blood before I was knocked out." Her hazel eyes are on the cement in front of us, a worrisome look about her. "She said she needed the blood of her enemy."

I can't even imagine what she'd been subjected to when Velda went rogue. Her anger toward the killer vamp must've been taken out on Hailey since she was the only other vamp around at the time. "I'm sorry," I tell Hailey, rubbing her arm as we continue up the sidewalk.

"You got her scent, though?" Julian asks me, grabbing my attention once more.

"Yes, I smell her."

I'd begun to naturally track her with Julian, and soon, our noses have led us up several other streets before we end up across the way from the woods.

Hailey's voice shakes timidly: "She went through there?"

We've been through these woods before, after surviving a horrible car accident together when the High Society had intentionally crashed into us to deter our progress in hunting them down. Is she having unsettling flashbacks as I am?

Not all of that night was unsettling, though. Especially the part when Julian fed me a bag of blood while he'd stared down at me with adoration. I'd gone too long without feeding and had become sick on our journey. I rather enjoyed him taking care of me. Or the part much earlier than that moment, when he'd hinted at being jealous upon learning that I didn't just feed from bags but from people... sometimes men. He didn't like the idea of me sinking my fangs into another man's neck. At the time, I couldn't understand his jealousy since he wasn't exactly offering up a vein (or his body in general). Quite the opposite, in fact – he'd seemed opposed to letting vamps feed on him. I grin thinking of how I'd tasted him as a vamp not that long ago, and he'd liked it. A lot.

Julian grumbles, a scowl forming. "Looks like it. I was hopin' this'd be easier. Guess nothin' ever is."

I look between him and the dark trees before us. "Something wrong?"

"I'll definitely lose her scent in there." He huffs. "Here's where we'll need help."

I blink up at him, smiling sweetly. "Time to howl?"

He grins. "Time to howl."

We hurry across the street, straight for the tall pines, the rush of wind and rain whipping their branches against one another harshly. Between the enormous trunks, past the brush and over the fallen branches and moistened land, we walk with purpose. Determination. Until Julian stops, looking up at the blackened sky shrouded with clouds pouring their angry tears down upon us. Not even the moon can be seen. I suppose I imagined him howling up at it. Now I'm a little disappointed not to witness something so dramatic... and probably quite sexy.

I wait in a nervous anticipation for him to actually get to the howling, moon or no moon.

A rumble deep in his chest sounds out, just as he takes a deep breath and releases it with an animal-like howl. My eyes widen in surprise hearing the sound, not expecting it to sound so wolf-like coming from a man. But he isn't a man... not exactly. I place a hand over my throat. Is that what I'll sound like?

Julian eyes me. "Give it a try."

"Howling?" I croak.

He chuckles, "Yeah." He smiles warmly at me. "Go on. Just inhale, think about what you want, and let your wolf voice speak."

"My wolf voice...," I laugh. It sounds so silly. But I must try. I'm like Julian now. I too can howl. Isn't it in my nature? Shouldn't it come naturally, just as tracking had? I shake off the uncertainty, the self-consciousness making my heart flutter, as I inhale as Julian instructed, thinking of my need to find Velda and how I require assistance. I open my mouth, lean my head back, and breathe out a howl just as Julian had.

I touch my throat again after, impressed with myself. Had I really just made such a sound?

"Nice," Hailey comments, grinning at me.

"Thanks."

In the distance, another howl is heard, one I estimate is at least a mile – perhaps two – away.

Someone's answered us. And not just anyone. Another wolf. I guess I didn't expect that either, an actual response. Somehow, I understand the howl. I know they're telling us they can help.

"Any idea who that is?" I ask Julian.

"Marv."

The bar owner I'd met once before? "You can really tell that?"

"It's not the first time we've spoken as wolves. I know his howl, just like I know his voice."

I whistle, impressed. "Impressive."

"Who's Marv?" Hailey asks.

I smile fondly. "A friend."

"Guess we're goin' to the bar," Julian states, carrying on. "We can get there through the woods."

And we do. We trek through the dark woods, past the creatures who eye us with suspicion, fear, confusion or curiosity. They shy away from us, retreating or keeping hidden from their spot within bushes. They remain tucked away between branches or playing hide-and-seek behind a trunk. Do they know what we are? Or do they simply sense we're dangerous? Hailey is a predatory species. Aren't wolves as well?

Perhaps they sense that from us, just as I sense the array of emotions coming off them. We travel quickly, our inhuman speed unmatched by those who watch us. Even if a fox or bear did spy us and hope for a snack, neither could hope to keep pace, let alone catch us.

Soon, we've arrived at the edge of the parking lot to Marv's, a security light at the back of the establishment lighting up the back entrance and a portion of the saturated lot. Only a few vehicles are back here. Staff, I imagine. The three of us hide behind a large green trashcan, surveying the lot. The rain has stopped, but our clothes remain soaked from travelling through the storm.

A classic country song plays within those brick walls. Laughter and conversation merges with the music. And as a scent wafts in my direction, one that calls to me and makes my mouth water and my stomach clench and rumble, I remember all too painfully the feeling of *hunger*. Not a thirst for blood. Not a gum-throbbing demand to feed. This is human hunger, the kind that takes me back to a life once lived in poverty, never knowing if a meal was my last or how long it'd be before the next one. Agony. It'd been agony starving.

Hailey looks at me when my stomach produces an excruciating growl. "Are you... hungry?"

I sadly nod.

Julian takes my hand in his and stands straighter, walking us toward the back entrance. "Let's get some food in you."

I don't have to go hungry here. Do I? As a vamp, feeding came easily. I could take it from anyone willing enough. And there were always humans who more than willingly sought to be fed from. Especially at Club Vudu. As a wolf, I'll require sustenance not so easily attainable, won't I? I recognize the trembling dread in my stomach, the one that isn't the discomfort of hunger. I'm afraid... afraid of starving again. Will that time ever come? I shake off that fear as we reach the door leading inside Marv's. I'm not human as I once was. I'm a werewolf. I can find prey in the very woods we'd just been in to eat.

...Although feeding off a cute and fuzzy animal doesn't appeal to me in the slightest. I'd much rather relish in the fried goodies that wait for me just beyond this door.

Julian turns and pulls on the knob, opening the door in our direction, allowing Hailey and myself to enter ahead of him into the kitchen.

"Hey!" someone complains, startling me. "You can't be back here!" His brows pull in further upon seeing Hailey. He points his greasy spatula at her. "Especially you, vampire!"

Offended, she scoffs.

It's then that I feel unwelcome, and not just because a room full of werewolf cooks are eyeballing us with both confusion and disapproval. I'm suddenly very much aware of another party of wolves who might also be present inside the restaurant... wolves who not only won't take too kindly to us bringing Hailey here but who have already tussled with Julian once before and might intend to do so again.

An uneasy tremble creeps up my spine, landing in the pit of my stomach, diminishing my need for fries and a cheesy bacon burger, as I remember the brawl that recently took place between Julian and a few angry wolves who'd insulted my previous vampiric state. Right here that fight happened, at Marv's. Julian has since killed two of those said wolves, ones who'd come to my business in the city with the intent to rape and murder me as vengeance against Julian for defending me... but mostly for beating them up, I'm sure.

I tighten my grip on Julian's hand. "Perhaps this was a bad idea."

"They can get the fuck over themselves!" Julian shouts, glaring at the wolves, his eyes brightening in warning. "We're here to see Marv! I'll come through whatever fuckin' entrance I want!" He notices the spatula-wielding cook eyeing Hailey with malice. Julian aims a pointed finger at him. "And I'll bring whoever the fuck I want with me!"

The wolf scowls but turns around and continues to flip the burger patties he'd been cooking. ...Or burning, it would seem. Our sudden arrival interrupted him, causing one side of the patties to become blackened. I hardly care if they're burned. I'd eat every last one of them. I eye each sizzling patty as we pass by them, my mouth filling with saliva once more.

"Are we getting a table?" I ask.

"A table?" Hailey asks, surprised. "We have to find Velda."

Oh, right. How had I forgotten? Had my hunger really been that demanding of my attention? Is that normal? For a vamp, sure. Blood can be quite addictive and cause one to act impulsively. It calls to vamps, distracting them from everything else around them. But this isn't blood. It's just a few burgers. And fries. And... I catch sight of someone pouring cheese sauce over a basket of fries with chili already on top. *Chili cheese fries?!* I grab the front of my shirt in my fist – a plain white cotton one Julian let me borrow that I'd since tied off for a better fit – swallowing back the saliva and trying to clear my mind from food. Hailey's right – we need to find Velda.

I wonder what food tastes like as we enter the front of the restaurant, spying people eating their meals. I don't have to wonder for long, as the smell of each item is so overpowering that my tastebuds pick up the taste, making my stomach ache more painfully. And suddenly, I want to cry. I don't just want to – I do. I wipe at the tears, feeling utterly silly (and a little angry) by the fact that any have been produced at all. What is going on with me?

Julian stops at the bar, and I spot Patrick, an acquaintance of Julian's, wiping the counter down with a stained rag. He catches sight of Julian and immediately grumbles, his brows pulling down and a sneer forming on his lips. "Fuckin' kiddin' me?! You again?"

Julian smiles. "Good to see you too, dick."

"What do ya want now?" Patrick asks, slinging the rag over his shoulder and folding his arms in front of him. "Your vamp ain't been back here since the last time you was lookin' for him."

"I'm here for Marv. But first, get my girl a basket of fries."

Patrick's gaze finds mine, and the scowl he'd worn smooths out. "Geez, you okay?"

Julian looks at me now, seeing my eyes swimming with tears I imagine. He touches my face, his thumb skimming my chin. "You're crying."

"I'm hungry," I confess, closing my eyes and crying more. Embarrassment takes over, and I hide my face against Julian's chest. "I've no idea why I'm crying."

"Uh…" Patrick says. "Wasn't she a…? How? What? What the fuck?"

Julian's hands are at my back, rubbing me comfortingly. "You need to eat somethin.'" His tone changes from soothing to demanding as he barks an order: "Patrick. Fries. Now."

I hear Patrick leave the bar area with a grumble. Hailey is soon standing closer. "Is she okay?"

"She'll be fine. Just needs to eat somethin' real quick."

Another hand touches my back, one that's cooler than Julian's. Hailey. She wants to comfort me, too.

"Here," Patrick says, having returned. Something hits the counter. A paper tray of fries, perhaps? "Now is anyone gonna tell me what the hell is goin' on here? Last I checked, she was a vamp! Now she's got a heartbeat and a hankerin' for fries. Help me out, here."

"She's my mate," Julian answers, removing his hands from my back. I move away from his chest, looking up at him as we separate. He searches my eyes. "You gonna be okay while I go talk to Marv?"

I nod.

He kisses my forehead before he heads off, leaving Hailey and I to sit at the bar. I stare at the container of fries, noticing with pure delight that they're smothered in chili cheese sauce. I smile, my eyes widening, as I sit down on a stool and begin to pluck a fry from the basket. I look at it in awe for a moment, before I stuff it in my mouth and begin to chew, my eyes closing as I savor the salty flavors blending together, how soft yet crunchy the fry is, a satisfied *mmm* coming up my throat.

"Glad ya like 'em," Patrick comments.

I open my eyes to regard him once before I stare at the food again, eating more. "Thank you for the food." How will I pay for it? Will he be angry when he discovers I have no money on me?

"You're welcome." He lowers his voice, leaning closer on the bar counter, resting his elbows on it as he studies me. "How'd this happen?"

I know he's asking how I went from a vamp to a wolf. Do I want to tell Patrick the details of my transformation? How Julian bit me and I switched species as a result?

"Is it 'cause you're his mate like he said?" he asks.

I nod, continuing to eat the fries, my fingers becoming sticky and warmer from the sauce. Halfway through, I nervously and guiltily inform him of my financial situation. "I don't have any money on me."

"So?"

I watch Patrick, assessing his expression, only finding confusion. "I can't pay for these. But... I can come back. I have money. I just... I don't have any on me at the moment."

Confusion turns to amusement. He lets out a small laugh. "How 'bout we say this one's on me."

He doesn't care in the slightest that I can't pay? Is it because we're both wolves and wolves look after one another? Or is Patrick... nice? Taking pity on me, maybe? Especially after seeing me cry like a hungry toddler? I'd like to think he's just nice, but I remember all too well how he'd acted toward me when I was a vamp. He was shocked to think Julian would be romantically involved with me (even though we really weren't at the time, as much as I'd wished it). He claimed he didn't like fangs digging in his neck... and I suspected then, just as I do now, that he definitely wouldn't associate with vamps himself.

Julian returns with Marv. "Time to split," he says.

"Where you goin'?" Patrick asks, looking between the two of them. "What's goin' on?"

"We're lookin' for a friend," Julian answers, grabbing a fry from my basket and tossing it in his mouth. He looks at Patrick in annoyance as he chews. "Any other questions?"

Patrick sneers at him. "You're fuckin' rude, ya know that?"

Julian laughs. "I guess I should be nicer, huh? Seein' how you fed my girl." He sighs, looking Patrick in the eye. "Patrick, I'm sorry for bein' an asshole."

Patrick just looks taken aback now. His mouth hangs open as we leave the bar. Clearly that was out of character, Julian apologizing to him. Or was it Julian being nice? Perhaps both...

Marv accompanies us into the lot, rubbing his long, peppered beard as he does. He looks around, his eyes glowing a bright blue. "I thought you said she was lost."

I give him a quizzical look.

Then it hits me. Her scent. It's strong.

Is Velda... here?

Chapter 19. Vengeance is a Hungry Beast

Rustling to my left causes me to jump and change my stance from relaxed to on guard – my knees and elbows bent, spine stiff. A slight pinch around my gums and fingernails startles me as well, my fangs and claws coming out, though I don't dare take my focus away from the possible threat in the woods coming our way. It could be Velda, but it could also be a trap. Has the serial killer vamp gotten her? Are we too late?

Velda emerges from beyond the darkness wearing a black cloak that covers her from head-to-toe, her feet bare and muddy, her eyes glowing a startling blue, her paled complexion much more ashen than usual. I relax once more but only slightly. She's not dead, but she's not herself, either. Hailey warned us she'd used dark magick to find the vamp. What price did she pay this time? I doubt a bit of vampire blood was enough.

"I hear you search for us," she speaks, her voice strange... as if more than one voice speaks. Others are present: deep, ominous ones.

Is she... possessed? Aside from the mix of voices speaking, she'd said *us*. As if more than one person resides within her... or more than one being. What exactly has taken hold of her?

"Velda?" Hailey asks, taking a cautious step forward.

Velda's eerie eyes watch Hailey, causing her spine to stiffen. She takes a step back.

"Yes, she is here," Velda answers.

"The hell does that mean?" Julian bellows.

Precisely my question...

Velda stares at Julian now. "We have joined her in her hunt."

We?

I don't particularly like her eyes on him. But they're not exactly her eyes, are they? No... something's wrong. Fear travels up my limbs and spine, my nerves tingling and warning me of danger. She's definitely possessed.

"Did you find him?" I ask, needing the focus of whoever this is off Julian.

Those unsettling eyes find mine, sending chills through me and an all-consuming dread that settles in my gut uncomfortably and causes my now beating heart to race. I know this feeling. It's death. A gasp escapes me.

"Not yet," the voices respond. "But we never stop until our purpose is fulfilled."

Tired of the group convo (and quite frankly wigged out by talking to something clearly evil), I demand: "I want to speak to Velda."

"You must speak to us all."

My brows pull down angrily hearing that. "What did you do to her? ...Who are you?"

She lifts her arms, bending them at the elbows, palms up to the night sky. "We are *The Three*, the seekers of the damned, the collectors of lost and frightened souls, the greatest tormentors. We are shadows in a vessel, welcomed to serve a purpose."

Well, none of that sounds good. That uncomfortable gut feeling grows stronger, leaving me nauseated, my skin tingling, a coolness crawling over me. Am I... sweating? I wipe at my brow, a wetness on the back of my hand.

What has Velda gotten herself into? She must've been incredibly desperate to find the killer, possibly sacrificing her own soul to do so. "And what's the price?"

"This host has agreed to our terms."

"That doesn't answer my question," I seethe, a pinching in my gums coming on again.

Julian places a hand on my arm.

Velda folds her hands in front of her. "Tis not your concern."

"She's our friend! It *is* our concern!" I touch at my throat, surprised by the way I'd sounded, like my words had been a growl, a threat to these evil beings playing host in Velda's body.

Those creepy eyes narrow on me, my knees trembling and stomach churning under their unwavering and unsettling gaze. Julian steps in front of me, separating me from those vengeful eyes.

"What happens when you find the vamp she's lookin' for?" Julian asks.

I peer at Velda from behind Julian's bicep, seeing her lift her chin. "We collect."

Collect the vamp... or Velda too? "I don't like this," I whisper.

A breeze comes through, sticky yet cool, sending my curls forward around my face. As the wind picks up, becoming stronger and louder as it whistles and whooshes and sends leaves and debris over our shoes, the oversized cotton tee I'm wearing molds against my back. There's a whisper in this wind, an eerie groan of one that speaks to the trees, sending them into a frenzy, their branches trembling and leaves shaking straight off, falling around is in a swirling dance.

Velda grins wickedly. "I sense a darkness. He is here."

The vampire... I look behind me, sensing something else dark in our midst as well, the unsettling impending doom feeling causing my heart to sink and gut to clench.

After all this time of hunting and searching, of reaching nothing but dead ends and losing hope every time he'd snatched another girl's life away, the moment has come where we finally put an end to these murders.

Or... Velda will... with the help of *The Three*. And when she's done, she'll have to pay that price she'd agreed to. Unless... Perhaps if those who inhabit her don't kill the vamp, their deal will be null and void. What if *we* kill him instead, us wolves and Hailey? Then those using Velda's body will have to leave, their mission incomplete. They've been summoned for one purpose: kill the serial killer vamp. If they don't fulfill that purpose, won't they have to leave her body and return to where they came from?

I cling to Julian's arm, wanting to tell him my plan but knowing those inside Velda will overhear. As my mate, can't I communicate my plan without speaking? Before we'd even fully connected, merging our bodies as one, he'd sensed my fear the night I was attacked by wolves at my shop. Our connection is even deeper now. I will my mind to connect with his, focusing until it almost hurts, a dull pang made of determined concentration and projection forming in the center of my skull.

Julian... WE must kill the vamp, NOT The Three. It'll void Velda's contract if The Three are unable to fulfill their end of the deal.

Can he hear me?

Julian's back stiffens, his arm becoming rigid under my tight fingers, bumps beginning to form and spreading across his flesh, causing the dusting of dark hairs along his forearm to raise. I know my thoughts have reached him.

Julain's voice is clear in my mind, returning a message: *I'll do what I can. The Three might not let us get the chance to break their deal.*

The very leaves that have fallen crunch under the weight of someone's steps as they near the back of the bar, the sound obnoxiously loud as I wait for the vamp to show himself. As I listen intently, noting their slow and steady walk, I hear something else. Something strong and loud and gushing... pumping blood through veins. A heartbeat. Then more beats, all different, all just as deafening. More footsteps.

A darkness is coming, but it's not the one we expected.

Julian protectively changes his stance, now shielding me from a different threat, his tall and broad frame stationed between me and the wolves.

One of them comes into view from around the side of the bar, his stout form shadowed until the faint glow of the security light welcomes him, brightening his blonde locks that hang over his yellowed, glowing eyes. That pit that formed in my stomach upon seeing Velda's possession only grows larger upon seeing him... and the others. Their leader wears the same leather vest he'd worn the night he'd preyed on me and Julian, the night I was brought to Marv's for the first time following a lead on our killer vamp. We'd pretended to be a couple, Julian and I, so I'd be left alone at the bar. But our plan had backfired, and instead of being left alone, we'd been targeted by this pack just for being different, for being a wolf-vamp couple.

Mike. That's the name of the one now leading an angry mob, the one who'd started the fight at Marv's that night. After his wolves paid me a visit at Vixen the following night, ending up dead as a result, I'd dreaded this moment... the moment Mike sought revenge.

Flashes of two wolves staring me down in the middle of Vixen emerge within my mind, one of them grabbing me and biting me, the pain that'd been at my neck and shoulder a terrifying memory of how sharp a wolf's teeth really are.

Unfortunately for them, I'm not a vampire anymore... and my teeth are just as lethal as theirs. I watch them from behind Julian's bicep, baring my new set of teeth, a low growl crawling up my throat and coming out a deadly warning to those looking for a fight, their eyes all glowing to show their intention.

The yellowed gaze from Mike only brightens, his own fangs showing as he lets out his own growl upon seeing me.

"Looks like it's our lucky night," he says, an excited grin forming on his smug face.

Julian extends his arm forward, his palm up and facing them. "We ain't here to cause trouble, and you shouldn't be either."

Marv steps between us all, his own blue irises now bright. "I thought I said you weren't welcome here anymore."

Mike laughs at Marv, sizing him up as his gaze travels from his head to his toes and back up again in one sweep. He points at Julian. "We just want *him*."

Marv raises his voice, his anger and impatience showing: "Well ya ain't gettin' him!" He points his own thick finger at the wolf threatening Julian. "Your friends went after his mate! They got what they got! Let it be a lesson to all of you!" He eyes each of the wolves standing behind their leader, their stances less threatening as they hesitantly look between one another. "Ya go after another wolf's mate, ya deal with the deadly consequences!"

Mike growls loudly, his fists clenched at his sides as he eyes Marv with hatred. "A vamp and a wolf ain't got no business bein' together. She ain't no mate!"

Vamp or wolf, we're meant to be together. His prejudices cause a rage to build within me, my already pounding heart quickening and beating forcefully against my ribs. I try to step forward, my fangs bared and a growl beginning in my chest. But Julian steps sideways to stop me, holding me back with his arm in front of me, shielding me from their view with his large frame.

The wolf eyes me now, grinning. "There she is, little cunt."

Julian growls, his back becoming rigid under my palm.

That only makes the wolf laugh, his head tilting back with it and long canines showing. He studies Julian, still laughing. "She worth it, losin' your life?"

Julian's back rumbles with an inner growl. "Oh, I won't be the one losin' my life tonight."

"Enough!" someone shouts behind me. The voices of *The Three*.

A shiver travels up my spine as Velda walks forward, her bare feet stepping over the fallen leaves and small twigs scattered about the lot, crunches and snaps sounding out.

"You must leave," she demands, eyeing the wolves.

"The fuck is this?" Mike snorts, sizing Velda up now. He puffs his chest out. "This doesn't involve you, freak!"

"You have disrupted our purpose," she says calmly. "Leave now, before it is too late for you."

"You threatenin' me?!" he laughs, astounded. He looks at the wolves behind him, noticing they've begun to retreat. His laughter fades, confusion beginning to show on his face. Then anger. "Where you goin'?! We ain't leavin' till we have his head mounted on a fuckin' wall!" He turns to eye Julian, his forehead creased in anger from how tightly his brows have knitted. "You're mine, traitor!"

He takes a step forward, then another, coming toward me and Julian. But then he stops and clutches his throat, shock forming on his face as he looks at Velda. She's holding her hand out toward him. His biker boots lift off the ground, barely holding him up by the tips of them.

"I told you to leave," Velda says, still just as calm. "Now you will suffer the consequences of refusing my kind offer."

The rest of the wolves turn and run, leaving their leader to face his demise.

Wide-eyed and terrified, face turning purple, Mike stares at his attacker as strangled grunts come out of him.

This isn't right. I might not know much about Velda, but this doesn't seem like her. She doesn't seem like a killer. The beings possessing her have taken over. She wouldn't want this… would she?

"Wait!" I shout, watching Velda's back, seeing Mike's frantic eyes now on me, pleading for help. "Don't kill him. This isn't what Velda would want! You came to kill the vamp. Not him. Let him go." Mike shuts his bloodshot eyes in agony, making strained sounds of protest as *The Three* clench their outheld fist now, strangling him further. "Please," I beg. "Velda! I know you're in there. Please stop! This isn't you!"

Suddenly, Velda drops her hand, and Mike falls to his hands and knees on the gravel, clutching his throat, coughing and gasping for air.

She turns to face me, eerie blue eyes turning red around the edges, opening that pit in my stomach wider, causing me to stumble back.

The voices are deeper now, angrier: "You."

"M-me?"

Julian's still in front of me, walking back with me as I stumble in escaping that frightening gaze.

"You threaten our alliance," they seethe, their voices all deeper now, her teeth clenched as she takes a step toward us.

Julian growls in warning, and Velda stops, her red-rimmed blue eyes darting to his. "Is it worth it, wolf?" they ask.

Julian eyes her back. "Is what worth it?"

"Losing your life. Are you willing to die for her?"

He looks back at me, sadness and love melting together in his eyes. He faces Velda, or rather, *The Three,* again. There's certainty in his voice: "Hell yeah."

They narrow their eyes on him, then me, before turning and walking toward the woods.

I'd been holding my breath waiting for their move, petrified of what they'd do to either of us. To both of us. Now, it rushes out of me in relief.

Julian breathes out his own sigh of relief. "Wh-what the hell?"

"Thought they were gonna kill you," Marv says, watching Velda disappear, his eyes widened in both surprise and horror. "The hell was that about?"

Julian stares at the trees, at emptiness now that Velda has disappeared. "...I don't know."

He turns to face me now, reaching out to gently grab the tops of my shoulders, pulling me into him, holding me captive against his chest, his large hands spanning the entirety of my back, his arms cocooning me. I wrap my arms around him, leaning in, breathing in his warm scent, memorizing the sound of his beating heart, thankful *The Three* didn't take his life. ...But why, exactly, did they ask him if he was willing to die for me?

"The fuck was that thing?" Mike asks, his voice shaky and raw. We turn to face him, seeing haunted eyes and a slack mouth as he stares at the trees, too. "She was suckin' the life outta me."

"I'd say that's what ya get," Marv grunts. "Now get!" he yells. "I don't wanna see your ugly ass face 'round here again, ya hear?!"

Mike's brows furrow as he glares at Marv. Then he looks at Julian. "This ain't over. You're gonna pay for what you did!"

I pull out of Julian's embrace, eyeing Mike with venom. I show my fangs just as my claws come out. Mike's eyes widen again as he takes in the sight of me wolfing out. "You kill my mate, and I'll tear you apart... slowly."

"The... the fuck?!" Mike stammers. "You're... you're a..."

"A wolf," I growl, taking a step toward him.

Hailey hisses next to me, her fangs out as she angrily eyes Mike.

Mike stumbles back, his eyes darting between us, before he disappears around the building.

I hope that warning was enough to make him stay away from us. But if not, we'll go after him just like we did Denise. We'll be left with no choice, after all.

Julian chuckles behind me.

I turn, seeing amusement in his eyes and upturned mouth. "What?"

"I'm impressed. You scared the hell outta him." He walks up to me, taking my chin between his thumb and forefinger, looking down upon me as I look up at him. "You're incredibly sexy right now."

Now it's my turn to grin. I lean up, staring at his lips, wanting nothing more in the world than to kiss him.

But someone grunts, interrupting the moment.

I turn to see Marv scratching the top of his peppered hair, his eyes on the sky. "We should get back inside. Forget about the girl... or uh... demon chick. She'll kill us all."

"No," Hailey protests, walking between us all, determination in her eyes. "We have to save Velda." She looks at the woods. "But it's obvious to me that we're outnumbered... by whatever's possessed her. I've called for backup." She glances down at her phone. "Or... uh, text for it."

"Who?" I ask.

"Derick. He knows someone who can help. A hunter."

Chapter 20. Catching Demons

We wait inside Marv's for Derick and this hunter friend of his to show. The three of us (myself, Julian and Hailey) sit at a booth, the wooden table before us unpainted and chipped to hell from years of wear and tear, the protective coating painted upon it shining brilliantly from the generic rectangular light fixture hanging above us. I grab a cheesy fry from the basket Julian just got for me and eye the steaming yellow goop dripping from it onto the paper tissue holding them all in place within a red plastic basket. Julian, I notice, eyes me from across the booth with a grin.

"What?" I laugh.

His grin deepens, exposing that adorable right-cheek dimple. "Nothin'. You're just cute, sittin' there eatin' your cheese fries."

"Admittedly, I've never tasted anything so good before."

Patrick swings by the table and settles himself in a wooden chair on the edge, the back of the chair facing our table as he plops down on it, legs spread to accommodate the position he's chose to sit in. "Even better than blood?"

Julian's grin disappears, replaced by a scowl as he glares at Patrick. "There a reason you came over?"

Patrick ignores Julian, instead focusing on me, his eyes narrowing as he looks me up and down. "I'm curious... how did this happen again?"

I shrug. "It's a mate thing."

Refusing to accept my simple answer, Patrick prods me further: "I mean, did you guys have sex, and then you just turned?"

Julian leans forward in the booth, the torn green plastic-covered cushion protesting beneath him as he does. He keeps his voice barely tame in what seems an attempt not to yell: "That's none of your damn business! Now get!"

Patrick scrunches his nose up at Julian before leaving, walking back to the bar with frustrated purpose.

Julian grumbles, "Disrespectful little shit." He looks at me, his furrowed brow smoothing out. "Sorry 'bout that."

I eye Patrick's back, feeling a little sorry for the guy. He's burning with curiosity. Anyone would be, desperate to know how a vampire can turn into a werewolf. "It's okay. He just wants answers."

"He shouldn't be askin' you about your sex life."

I turn to face him now, raising a brow at that. Man has a valid point. "You're right about that." Hailey's busied herself next to me texting Derick on-and-off the last ten minutes. I eye her next. "Are they nearly here?"

"Almost."

I finally eat the fry I've been holding, licking my cheese-coated fingers after. "So... what kind of hunter is this person?"

Summoned right on time, Derick walks into Marv's, another man at his left. No, not a man. A vampire. A vampire... hunter? Just a hair taller than Derick, but much darker than the ashen vamp I know, he walks with confidence, standing tall as he looks around the bar, his brown eyes lighting up just the smallest bit, turning them a warm amber, when he takes in the majority of the clientele, undoubtedly sensing their werewolf state. His thick, black hair is gelled, a mohawk running from the front to the back of his head. A white tee fitted perfectly against his muscular frame is covered partially by a faded black leather jacket. Faded black jeans, fitted just as well as his tee, cover his legs. Black moto boots are on his feet, scuffed-up and muddied, the front of one (on his fight foot) having developed a small hole from such excessive wear. Or is that a bullet mark? I narrow my eyes to get a closer look, uncertain upon further inspection, what the cause could be.

Derick catches sight of Hailey, a smile immediately forming on his lips. I turn to see Hailey's entire face lighting up upon seeing Derick – her eyes widening just slightly, her brows raising noticeably as well. Her lips even part just the smallest bit. Hailey slides out of the booth to greet her vampire fiancé, embracing him with a tight hug just as he's reached our table. He closes his eyes and leans into her, wrapping both his arms around her, his nose buried in the side of her neck.

"Missed you," he whispers.

"I missed you, too," she whispers back, holding him tighter.

"Derick," Julian says, sliding out of the booth as well to stand and greet his friend and this hunter stranger. "Thanks for comin' out." He looks at the hunter, offering his hand to him for a friendly shake. "Name's Julian. Appreciate you takin' the time to help us out."

The vampire shakes Julian's hand tentatively, looking into his eyes curiously. Is he nervous to be helping a werewolf?

The vampire hunter's voice is deep and gruff, with the smallest hint of a southern accent: "No problem. I hope we can rid the world of these demons soon enough. Name's Jesse. Jesse Jackson."

Their handshake ends, just as Derick and Hailey part.

Derick shakes Julian's hand next. "Hey, man. Heard all about your demon problem." He nods toward Jesse. "Jesse specializes in hunting, trapping and sending them back to whatever hell dimension they came from."

Julian nods slowly, eyeing Jesse. "You hunt anythin' else?"

Jesse's eyes narrow as he watches Julian in return, his lips twitching as a grin threatens to come on. "If you're asking me if I hunt werewolves, no. Just demons. There are a great number of them inhabiting the earth. I'm just doing my part to expel them."

Still sitting in the booth, my exit blocked by Hailey standing between me and my freedom, I watch Jesse just as curiously as he'd watched Julian before. "How do you send them back to a hell dimension?"

Jesse's eyes are on mine now. "A spell."

That's all? "It can't be that simple."

He chuckles. "Never is. I'll have to tranquilize your friend so her body is unconscious. The demons within will still be able to hear me chant. They'll fight the summoning spell, knowing it's a trap. If all else fails, taunting them to lure them out often works."

"Taunting them?" I ask.

His grin deepens, his fangs showing. "You'll see. For now, we should all get going. Go find this friend of yours. Tranquilize her. Start the spell. Catch some demons. Rid the world of a little evil." He slaps his hands together and rubs them, an excited smile forming on his lips. "Shall we?"

I sense this is how he gets his jollies – hunting demons. But why? Does it keep him from embracing his vampiric side and hunting humans? Or is he truly only interested in ridding the world of evil, one pesky little demon at a time?

"Where to?" Jesse asks, looking between us all.

I've no clue where Velda might have gone, but perhaps starting from the beginning wouldn't hurt. Landon might be awake by now, and he might know something.

"Wix," I suggest.

Having arrived on foot to Marv's, two wolves and a vamp now sit in the backseat of Jesse's *classic* Range Rover while Jesse drives. Derick sits shotgun. Quite frankly, this vehicle is just as disintegrated as the man's boots: the tan paint chipping off the rusted sides and the door hinges squeakier than the entrance to a haunted house. To my surprise, a *put, put* hasn't followed us to Velda's shop... though we have experienced a bit of a roller coaster ride upon hitting even the smallest bump in the road along the way, our bottoms lifting off the seats each time we've run over one or hit a chughole. If not for the scented green pine tree hanging from his rearview mirror, the stench of mold would be much more overpowering.

As I sit between Hailey and Julian, I catch sight of a spatter of orange dried to the back of the passenger seat. "What's this?"

"You're gonna have to be a bit more clear," Jesse responds.

I pick at the orange stain with my fingernail. "This orange stuff stuck to the back of your seat here."

"Oh, just a demon I killed last week."

I quickly pull my fingers back. "Ew." He couldn't have cleaned it off?

He laughs, "Yeah, I thought she was really into me, but all she wanted was my collection of medieval knives I'd talked about at the bar I met her at."

"How charming," I comment with a sarcastic grin.

"Could've been an epic romance...," he muses.

I raise a brow. "Thought you killed demons, not kissed them."

He glances over his shoulder at me. "Is that judgement I'm detecting?"

I shrug. "Just saying..."

He chuckles, "I was bored and drunk. Thought it'd be fun." He grunts, clearing his throat. "It wasn't."

Jesse parks in front of Velda's shop. Inside, the lights have been cut. Is Landon still inside? We'd left the poor lad unconscious with nothing but a note describing our whereabouts and Velda's.

Julian exits the vehicle first, holding his hand up as soon as his boots have touched the cement outside his door. "Stay in here," he tells me. "Let me check things out first."

He shuts the door, and I watch as he walks up to the entrance of Wix, peering inside through the glass. That's when we all see the glowing neon green light emitting from within the shop.

Jesse gets out, then, sword in hand.

...Where'd that sword even come from?

Hailey leans forward, watching them as she speaks to Derick: "Should we...?"

He keeps his eyes forward, watching them approach the entrance. "I'm not sure. Don't want to get in Jesse's way."

"Won't he need our help?" I ask. Julian opens the shop door, and he and Jesse walk in. "I'm not comfortable staying here." I get out of the Range Rover, ignoring Julian's instructions he'd given me. That green light is obviously supernatural, and I refuse to end up mate-less simply because I'd done as I was told by staying put.

"Ivy, wait!" Hailey hisses after me, having gotten out of the SUV as well. Her perturbed gaze is on Wix, the green light coming through the glass windows so bright now that her tan complexion is glowing eerily from it. "I'm coming with."

Derick's already joined her at her side. "Me, too."

I grab the shop door handle and pull, opening the glass door and waltzing in with my vamp friends, my own claws out just as surely as their fangs are. The entire place is lit up by this unnatural neon green color, its origin the backroom where Velda does her spells.

What did she do now?

Landon's gone.

Grunting and screaming has us running toward that door. I fling it open, first blinded by the green light, then sent back a step from a gust of air crashing into me, my clothes ruffling from the impact and hair blowing past me in frenzied waves. Before me stands Jesse, yelling as he holds a box open, a screeching dark shadow being sucked into it. His sword is on the floor, its blade just as shiny and unstained as it'd been when Jesse walked in with it. Velda is unconscious on the black tile floor. On his knees beside her, cupping her face and pleading for her to survive, is Landon. My eyes dart all over the room, finally finding what I seek: Julian, lying face down in a corner.

"Julian!" I shout over the whooshing wind and shrieking shadow demon. Is he just knocked out? Or is he...?

No, he can't be. I'd have *felt* that.

I take a step in his direction, but Jesse casts me a warning glare, yelling: "Stay back!"

I halt, my widened eyes watching in horror as the demon shadow lets out a final, deafening scream before being sucked into the box, the lid being forced shut by Jesse. Jesse stumbles backward after, holding the box between his hands with force, grunting as he tries to keep it closed.

"Decipula!" he demands, the wind around us ceasing just as Jesse relaxes his grip on the box. He lets out a huff. "Damn thing didn't wanna go in there." He grins down at the object. "Enjoy each other's company, lads."

I eye him and the black box half the size of his hand, giving him an incredulous look. "I thought you were sending the demons back to a hell dimension, not trapping them in a box!"

Jesse raises a single dark brow, huffing a laugh. "It's a process." He turns the box over in his hand, the action showing the silver pentagram design on one side.

I walk past him, making my way to Julian, my knees hitting the hard, cold floor as I assess him, my hands on his back. "Julian." I shake him some. "Wake up." He grumbles but remains still. I gently shake him again. "Should I be worried?"

"No," he mumbles.

A relieved breath leaves me. Although I'm grateful he's okay, I'm upset that he'd risked his life at all. I glare at the back of his head, frustrated now. My hand comes down on his back with a *smack*. "You could've gotten yourself killed!"

"Ow!" he protests. He grunts before moving to get up, soon sitting before me, his hand coming up, a couple fingers rubbing at his temple. Eyes still closed, he winces from touching his head.

"Are you hurt?" I ask, leaning forward, touching his temple with the softest touch I can manage, the tips of my fingers barely making contact against his skin.

He opens his eyes, blinking rapidly, finally settling them on mine, his pained expression softening. "Got thrown across the room is all. I'll be fine."

"What happened?"

Jesse answers: "Had to use him as bait." I turn to find Jesse standing over Velda, looking down at her with his hands on his hips. "Two down, one to go."

"What do you mean you used him as bait?!" I demand.

Jesse looks at me, then Julian, a smirk forming. "Needed someone to distract the demons while I tranquilized her."

I open my mouth to fire back at him for using *my* mate as bait, but Julian puts his hand on my shoulder.

"Did what we had to do," he tells me.

I face him again. "You could've been killed."

He shrugs. "Nah. Velda wouldn't let 'em kill me." He chuckles, "Besides, I'm kinda hard to kill."

I'm not finding the humor in this situation. "Werewolf or not, we're up against demons. Don't underestimate them."

"She's right," Jesse inputs.

I couldn't care less about getting his approval. I stand up, helping Julian to his feet as well, before glaring at Jesse again. "Your methods are messy."

"Catching demons isn't exactly clean," he retorts.

He's still standing over Velda. "Now what?" I ask.

Jesse eyes me. "Now we catch the last one."

"How?"

He looks at the black box he'd set down on a shelf housing jars and herbs. "Can't use that again. Need something..." He looks around the room, his eyes darting from shelf to shelf.

"Like?"

"An object... something small and solid. Nothing translucent. Glass doesn't hold demons, not even the colored kind. Neither does ceramic."

"What does?"

He shrugs. "Metal. Plastic. Leather. Something we can close, like a box."

Hailey reaches into her purse, pulling out a reusable plastic bottle. "Something like this?"

Jesse holds his hand out, and Hailey gives it to him. He opens the bottle and brings it to his nose, taking in the scent of the contents housed inside the container, his fangs lengthening as he does. He eyes Hailey. "You gonna miss this?"

The coppery smell hits me, then. Blood.

"No," she answers. "I can get more."

I point at the bottle, suddenly thinking my words just as I say them: "Isn't it a bad idea to mix blood with a demon? Won't that... do something?"

Jesse looks from me to Hailey. "Is this sacrificial blood?"

She makes an uncertain face. "I mean... I got it from a willing donor. I didn't, like, kill for it."

"Or perform a ritual?" Jesse asks.

Her brows shoot up. "Goodness, no!"

Jesse looks at me again. "Guess it's fine, then."

I eye him madly. "You *guess* it's fine?!"

He laughs, as if all of this is amusing to him. "You're overthinking things."

My back stiffens, hands beginning to clinch at my sides. "I think I'm thinking things through quite necessarily! Perhaps *you* should think *more*!"

He continues to grin. "I've been doing this for centuries. I'm pretty sure I've got this. You can go wait in the car..."

I open my mouth, fury taking over and about to spill out of me, but Julian grabs my arm before I can stalk toward Jesse.

"Let's just save Velda," he tells me, his voice soft. "That's what we came here for." He glares at Jesse, his tone harsher: "Do your damn job so we can get the fuck outta here."

Chapter 21. Saving Velda

Jesse holds the open plastic bottle in front of him, arm outstretched as far as possible toward Velda. He eyes her unmoving form on the floor. "Prodire," he demands, waiting then, as the rest of us do, for his words to bring forth the last demon.

After silence passes us by – several seconds worth – my shoulders relax. "Should something be happening?"

Jesse's thick brows come down as he continues to stare at Velda. "This one's being stubborn." He changes his stance, his legs widening, both hands now on the black plastic bottle as he holds it out toward Velda. "Maybe it's a coward."

"A coward?" I ask.

"Yeah," Jesse says slowly, grinning. "A real weak link. Has to hide behind little girls. Can't do anything on its own. That sorta coward."

I eye Velda as her body twitches. Is he... *taunting* the demon to get it to come out? He'd mentioned at Marv's that taunting demons was one way to get them out. Does he think this will actually work, though? Insulting it?

"Guess I shoulda known it'd be too afraid to face me." He snorts, "Can't even do the one thing it was summoned to do."

Suddenly, the air becomes chilled, prompting me to wrap my arms tightly around myself, an uncomfortable shiver travelling throughout my body, leaving me trembling. My breath comes out in puffs from my quivering lips.

A swirl of black and red smoke appears around Velda's middle as the demon emerges, the crimson color flickering angrily as if its lightening trapped within clouds. As though a storm has come through, a wind whips out from that smoke, sending my hair flying away from my face. I squint against the cold, dry air stinging my eyes, watching the swirling being grow even larger, its figure forming: long limbs made from smoke develop in twists as crooked horns grow from its enlarged head – a petrifying creature's form indeed. Even I take a step back, straight into Julian's warm embrace, who pulls me even farther back. Dread settles in the pit of my stomach just as tingles of warning travel through my nerves along my limbs.

This is absolute *evil*.

Ethereal red eyes stare down its tormentor – Jesse.

Jesse readies himself, chanting under his breath as his knuckles turn white around the bottle, his eyes set in determination on the demon. Over the constant *whoosh*, a whistle begins, sharpening and becoming louder, morphing into a screech. Jesse's lips are moving quickly, soundlessly over the wind and screams, the demon beginning to move toward him as he speaks.

As the screeching continues, I must cover my ears, the sound unbearably tormenting my drums, a sharp pain causing even I to fall to my knees with Julian. Jesse's ears have begun to bleed, but he doesn't stop chanting, nor does he fall as we have. His focus is unwavering on the demon. Just as the demon begins to be pulled into the bottle, Jesse struggles to maintain his footing, as though the malevolent creature is pulling him toward itself. It's a tug-of-war. A vein protrudes from Jesse's neck as his face goes from deep red to nearly purple, the glistening redness travelling along his flesh from his bleeding ears saturating the collar of his white tee as he chants on, teeth grit.

As the bottle shatters, bits of plastic and blood fly throughout the room, and the demon gives a final screech before it breaks free from Jesse's spell and flies toward the door of the room, leaving us in the eerie quiet aftermath of a war.

My hands fall from my ears. Jesse's eyes are incredibly large as he stares at the open door, his jaw hanging open, the last of the busted bottle still in one of his hands.

I look between him and the door, disbelief evident in my tone: "Did... did it just get away?!"

Jesse's silent, his eyes still staring after the now gone demon.

"Jesse?" Derick asks.

Jesse blinks.

"Jesse!" Derick shouts, causing Jesse to blink rapidly back into the present.

"I...," Jesse begins. "I... That's never happened before."

"Well now what?!" I demand. "We have to go after it!"

He shakes his head, his jaw clenched. "Not *we*. Me."

"No," Velda says. We all turn to look at her as she begins to slowly stand up. Landon keeps his hands on her shoulders, ensuring she doesn't fall over. She's hunches slightly, clearly weak from being possessed and then unpossessed. She takes a steadying breath, her eyes glistening with tears of remorse, dark shadows beneath them. "Me."

"No offense, little witch," Jesse says, looking her up and down. "But demon hunting doesn't exactly look like your forte." He points the busted piece of blood-stained plastic still between his thumb and forefinger at her. "You're the reason we're in this damn mess."

She lifts her chin. "Precisely. Only I can undo this."

"How?" Landon asks her, worry evident in his green eyes as he studies her.

Velda looks at Hailey. "Claire. She's connected to it. She can help me."

Hailey's haunted eyes are on Velda's. "Claire?"

Velda's glistening blues remain on Hailey, her brows sadly pulling in. "She warned me. She came to me as I did the spell, telling me of a break between dimensions that would grow even weaker if I carried on with my plan." She closes her eyes tightly, the tears that'd been swimming in them now cut off and left to cascade rapidly over her paled cheeks. "She told me you'd bore witness to this demon's power before."

"When?" Hailey asks.

Velda's voice is hollow: "During the séance."

My face cools as though blood's drained from it, a pricking of needles playing at my skin. I remember all too well my run-in with a force on the stairs in Vixen's basement. Claire had warned us to run from something when we'd reached out to her during the séance... and I'd been caught on the staircase as I'd heeded her warning and tried to escape, the breath unexpectedly knocked out of me. The feeling of death and dread was just as consuming of my frame then as it had been moments ago when I'd looked upon that demon. Our séance had *invited* it into our world. And now... I look at the open door it'd flown out of with horror. Now that thing is free to roam the streets.

Barely a whisper, my voice breaking around the words: "What will this demon do now that it's free?"

"Collect souls," Velda answers. "Like Claire's. She's..." Her sorrow is evident as more tears form within her eyes, her voice low and raw with it: "She's one of its victims. It feeds on terror. It's drawn to it. And her... her murder was so horrific, her fear so profound, it'd been summoned to the scene and collected her soul as she died. And since this demon has been trying to break free from its hell dimension, collecting more and more souls to do so, any souls connected to it were able to come through, too." Her eyes are on Hailey again. "That's why Claire could speak to you. And that's what she's been trying to warn you about. The demon counted on your pain and guilt and Claire's pain and guilt to bring itself closer to our world. The closer it is, the more terror it senses, and the more souls it can collect. Once it collects enough souls, it can walk among men, taking possession of whomever it so chooses."

"We invited it," I say, swallowing back a lump in my throat. "When we did the séance."

Hailey and I exchanged horrified looks.

"No," Velda guilty admits. "I invited it. I ignored Claire's warning. I thought I could control the entire situation. My vengeance blinded me, made me make a terrible choice."

Hailey's eyes drift to the floor, silence ensuing again. I think back on the séance, remembering Claire talking about purgatory, how in order for her soul to be set free, she needed to complete trials.

"But what about the trials?" I ask aloud, looking from Hailey to Velda. "Claire said she could be free if she completed trials. If her soul has been collected, how can she ever hope to escape? What trials would there even be?"

Velda thinks on that for several moments, her brows creasing deeper with each passing second. "It must be a loophole. Like with spells... there's always a way to undo something or get out of something. What if this demon's sentence is to collect souls until it can walk among men, but the souls it collects can be freed if they truly desire it, leading to this demon always having to work for its own freedom, too. For every soul that frees itself, it must collect more and more... a vicious cycle. A way for things to stay balanced." Her eyes widen. "A way to keep the demon from actually walking among men. And I'd..." Her jaw is left open, her eyes growing wider. "I broke the cycle. I gave it full access to our world."

"Fuck," Jesse mutters. "This is a million times over, fucked!" He pinches the bridge of his nose, closing his eyes tightly as he does. "You're right. *You* set it free. *You* opened the gate. *You* have to close it."

Velda wipes away tears with the backs of her fingers, lifting her chin as much as she can manage. "And I will."

Chapter 22. The Wedding

One Month Later

What a glorious, sunshiny day. Despite it being December, it's still quite warm out in Texas. A few clouds occupy the sky, each of them dissolving into separate pieces, forming new shapes I stare up at, deciphering them. One looks a lot like an eerie shadow, its eyes and mouth widening as the cloud moves, opening up to swallow me whole. Since shadow demons are fresh on my mind, it's no wonder that's what I see. I tear my eyes away from the dissipating makeshift shadow demon, focusing them on Julian instead. Dressed in a black tux, he's pulling at the tie around his thick neck with a grimace. I smile warmly at him, entertained by his disapproval of the required wedding attire. He prefers jeans and tees.

I play with the necklace he'd given me last night that now sits around my neck, the black, heart-shaped pendant with a white crescent moon etched on the front perfectly outlined under my fingers. *"You'll always be in my heart,"* he'd said, as he'd secured it around my neck several hours ago. I haven't taken it off since, not during our pleasant romps, not as we'd slept, and not even as I'd showered this morning before getting ready for the wedding. And I don't intend to ever take it off... unless of course we're wolves running through the woods. Julian promised we'll do that soon. As much as I'm excited about turning into a wolf, I'm nervous about the transition itself... how it'll feel during it all, how I'll fare running on four legs, etc.

He smiles when he sees me eyeing him, noticing I'm playing with the pendant. Does he know where my thoughts are, scattered as they may be? As his irises flicker gazing upon me, one thought races forward, causing my beating heart to accelerate and blood to run faster through my veins.

"Don't worry," I huskily whisper, nodding at his tie. I take a step forward, now standing in front of him in the satin red bridesmaid dress that hugs my figure perfectly. I look up at him, a seductive grin on my lips. "I assure you that you won't be wearing that suit for long."

He pauses in loosening his tie. He looks around the lot outside the church, one currently full of vamps and wolves who can all hear (whether I'm whispering or not) the daring thing I've just said. His face even turns pink just before he clears his throat, looking over my figure hungrily. "I look forward to it."

His irises are ablaze, their color more green than blue today, the reflection of my own gleaming amber eyes showing in his dilating pupils.

"Hey, love birds," a familiar voice says.

I gasp, turning around quickly to find Madison standing behind us, baby Allie on her hip.

"Madison!" I squeal, giving her and Allie a hug. I take Allie's chubby pale hand in my own, her little fingers squeezing my index finger happily. As I coo at her, a giggle escapes her, and she bounces on Madison's hip.

Dorian walks over with Landon, joining Madison's side.

Landon's brows are pulled down heavily, his focus shifting as he scans the lot. "Have you seen Velda? I swear she's here, but... I can't find her."

I glance around the lot as well. "Nope. I know she's coming, though. We got her a dress so she could be a bridesmaid, too." I wink at him. "She tried it on last night. You might literally fall over when you see her in it."

Landon's eyes brighten a stunning green as a smile forms on his mouth, dimples on each cheek deepening.

I continue to coo at Allie, leaning close to take in the smell of baby powder, linen and innocence (a comforting scent, like chrysanthemums warmed by sunshine). She makes a pleased baby scream, causing several guests to turn and smile at her.

"You're just the sweetest wittle wolf baby there ever was," I coo, practically bursting from joy watching her fuss in pure happiness, more squeals emerging from her.

Dorian looks between me and Allie, then grins at Julian. "Uh oh."

Julian laughs.

I look between the two of them, seeing some kind of secret exchange occurring. "What?"

Dorian laughs now, "Just looks like you might be wanting one of your own soon."

Warmth spreads along my cheeks thinking of having an Allie of my own. Being a vamp for so long, I'd pushed away thoughts of having children. Since turning into a wolf, I've given having a family with Julian some thought, but we've only just begun our journey. "I... I'm..."

Julian puts a warm hand on my back. "We're not quite there, Dorian. Baby steps."

Dorian, still grinning, shakes his head. "Poor choice of words, my friend."

Julian shifts his feet. "Well now ya got me thinkin' 'bout babies."

Dorian chuckles, putting his arm around Madison's shoulders as he does. She gives a small chuckle back, but her mind seems elsewhere. Her attention is on the vast space above us, her baby blues bluer than ever as the brightly lit sky reflects off them.

What's she staring at?

I look up, too, wondering if the eerie cloud shape I'd seen is still visible. But it's not. "Something wrong?"

Madison looks at me now, her blonde brows pulling in. "Is it just me... or does something seem off today?"

"Off?" Julian asks.

She looks up again, her voice low and curious: "Strange, maybe..."

"I did see a creepy cloud shape earlier," I comment. "But I've been creeped out since... well, since that *thing* got released into the world." I don't dare say *demon* out loud. It'll jinx us all.

Dorian pulls Madison closer, tucking her and Allie into his side. "The demon..."

So much for not jinxing us by saying *that* word out loud. "Mm-hmm."

Now he looks up, seeming perplexed – his eyes crinkling with concern. "Let's go inside the church."

"There's holy water in there," Velda states, appearing seemingly out of nowhere next to me. I gasp and jump, my heart thudding uncomfortably in response to her sudden arrival. Addie's hold on my finger loosens as a result, her chubby hand now gone from mine. "Might come in handy. Besides," she says, holding up an empty glass bottle with a large bottom and thin long neck, "I need to restock."

"Where...?" I begin to ask, thinking better of it. She *is* a witch, after all. Probably just *poofed* herself here. "Never mind." I glance at the clear bottle in her hand. "Does holy water really work on evil things?"

She grins at me like she has a secret. "Of course."

She turns and heads toward the church entrance, and we all follow.

Landon rushes ahead, walking closely at her side. "Did you just get here? I swear I've felt you this whole time..."

Velda says nothing, but I do catch sight of a grin as Landon opens one of the two church doors, allowing her to enter ahead of him.

He's *felt* her this whole time? Is Velda truly Landon's mate? A wolf and a witch... how interesting would that be...

Inside the church, white roses decorate the ends of the pews, and a long red rug stretches out from the entrance to the alter, white rose petals scattered all over it. I inhale happily, taking in the delicate scent of the flowers and the woodsy smell of the polished pews. "Lovely. Just lovely."

"Yes, you are," Julian smiles.

I look up at him, seeing his bright eyes on me, my red lips stretching as my own smile forms.

We take our seats on the left side, with Allie between me and Madison, her white-stocking-clad chunky legs stretched out before her, little black Mary Janes adorning her feet. She occupies herself by playing with the pink silk ribbon around the waist of her lace dress.

"So, about this new pack," Dorian says, leaning forward from the left of Madison to see Julian to the right of me. "Do we have weekly meetings?"

Julian leans forward to see Dorian. "Weekly sounds good to me. We can have dinner."

"I can make a pot roast," Madison cheerily adds. "And I'll bring fresh blood for Derick and Hailey."

Two nights ago, we'd all gotten together – two vamps, five wolves and a witch – to talk about being in Julian's pack. A natural leader with a desire to lead us into a future of protecting each other and the humans, he'd called upon us all to join. And we'd all gladly accepted his offer. As far as we know, we're the first "pack" of more than just wolves. Hailey and Derick are vamps, after all... and Velda's a witch. But we all have the same goal, the same mission: Do what's right. Protect one another. Protect the weak (like the humans who are defenseless against supernatural's). Julian said he's never seen such a strong pack before, and he knows he can trust all of us, that we'll all contribute to the pack in special ways, making it more powerful than any he's ever been part of.

"What do we talk about in these meetings?" I ask.

Julian shrugs. "Anything. It doesn't have to be all business. But first things first, I do wanna go over our plan for a certain evasive vamp who keeps slippin' through our fingers." In front of us, Velda's shoulders tense. "Pretty soon, there ain't gonna be no more blondes in Pareen County... or the surroundin' ones, for that matter."

Velda turns around, and Landon mirrors her movement.

Her eyes are on Julian. "We'll find him." Her stare drifts, falling on the front of his tux, her brows worrisome. "I feel that we're so close. I'm just... missing something."

"How 'bout you just focus on that..." Julian looks at the giant wooden cross at the front of the church, "uh... shadow creature."

"Demon," Dorian corrects.

Julian shoots him a glare. "Stop sayin' that word, would ya?"

Dorian shrugs his massive shoulders, his tux jacket tightening around them from the movement. "What? That's what it is..."

Julian opens his mouth to say something else, but Derick shows up at the end of our pew. "You guys ready to come up front?"

We all scoot ourselves out of the pew, walking up front to stand where we're supposed to while we wait for Hailey. As we'd talked about our new pack, a serial killer vamp and a shadow demon on the loose, the church had filled up with all the guests. As I stand at the front of the church, a piano tune plays behind me, the bridal chorus I'm familiar with setting the scene perfectly. Everyone sitting in the pews turns to face the back of the church, waiting as we are for Hailey to appear. When she does, a few gasp upon seeing her in the white, lace gown that caresses the floor, the off-shoulder top revealing her shiny, tan shoulders. Behind the matching veil over her face, her hazel eyes settle on Derick, and her full, baby pink lips part with a smile that shows her pearly whites. Preacher Pete, a dear friend of mine, stands next to Hailey with a hunch in his posture, his arm within hers. He pats her hand, which is resting on his forearm, signaling that they can proceed. As Hailey begins to walk up the aisle, her eyes glisten with emotion as she watches Derick. I glance at Derick, seeing his do, too. He wears the same smile of excitement as her, their attention solely on one another; it's as though no one else is here – just them.

Hailey takes her place next to Derick, and they face one another, eyes still bright with passion and longing. Derick takes her hands in his, and Preacher Pete begins the ceremony. Behind Derick, Julian eyes me, a certain glint in his eyes. I know where his heart is, where his thoughts are, just as he senses mine. We see ourselves here someday, too... though our bond is already solidified. Humans (and vamps) have this type of ceremony to bind themselves to one another, to make vows and dedicate their life to their intended. Julian and I have already done so, our bond supernatural and destined. But it would certainly be nice to declare our love in front of our friends, would it not? Perhaps a wedding is definitely in order. Besides, Hailey's heart-shaped diamond ring she's been wearing is astonishing. I'd very much like my own, but perhaps in a teardrop shape.

After the wedding, we immediately head to the reception, a log cabin building tucked away in a wooded area, its large windows showcasing what's inside – several tables and chairs and floral arrangements. The area is surrounded by trees that have dangling, sparkling white lights hanging from their branches. It all looks quite magical and enchanting.

Once inside, warmed blood sits inside glass pitchers to feed those of us who are vampires. Disposable metal trays sit upon a table housing what appears to be chicken alfredo and salad contents. A couple containers even have lasagna. My stomach clenches with a sudden hunger. When shall we eat? I walk past the table of blood and food, into the room of tables with glorious centerpieces – a large clear jar holds a white vanilla scented candle atop each table, the glass encompassed by real wood branches that travel up its sides. Red rose petals are scattered across the cream-colored satin tablecloths. The dark wooden chairs all have matching cream bows strapped to their backs. Those in our group – myself, Julian, Landon, Velda, Madison, Dorian and Addie – take our seats at one of the tables. A low, romantic tune of violins and piano floats throughout the room.

I observe the guests taking seats at their own tables. I've never seen so many vamps and wolves together... actually having fun. It warms my heart seeing such peace among us all, different as we all are.

"Please, let's eat!" Hailey announces, still in her wedding dress, as she stands near the table of food and blood. "I'm starved!"

Laughter erupts, chairs slightly screech as people begin to stand once more, and heels and flat soles noisily make their way across the grey and white marble floor. We join the crowd, grabbing our own food. My plate is loaded with noodles, chicken and sauce. Julian grabs himself even more, taking both alfredo and lasagna, a hill forming of the two. I laugh as I observe his plate closely matches that of Dorian's.

Soon, we've all taken our seats and have begun to eat, the aroma of Italian spices overwhelming my senses just as powerfully as the taste. Soon, my belly is satisfied, and we hold conversations as the evening progresses.

We dance.

We mingle.

We have a blast.

Until a coldness fills the air, taking away our laughter, sucking all the joy out of the room and replacing it with anger... so much anger. Laughter and voices begin to fade as everyone registers the change in both temperature and temperament of our environment.

Then darkness shrouds us as the lights go out.

Some people scream and scramble to get to the Exit. Others try to stay calm, confusion and terror crossing their faces. Some stand around indifferent, as though they've faced worse. What's a little coldness... a little bit of malevolent anger in the air?

Those that are indifferent... they haven't faced a demon, have they? Have they ever beheld the evil and knee-buckling gaze of one as it stared them down?

I sincerely doubt they have, but they soon will, won't they? The demon has returned, and it's about to be a bloodbath.

The dread and terror swirling in my gut and chest intensifies as death takes hold of me… choking me, holding me captive in its grim grip. I open my mouth to let in air, but I cannot. Heart beating in tune to my panic, I grab at my throat, my knees weakening as I do.

Something crashes into me forcefully, allowing the air I'm so desperate to breathe in to finally fill my lungs. I *feel* her there, pulling me under, pushing me down, taking over. Her hatred is so heavy, weighing down both my heart and my will to move. I can't escape her wrath, her control.

Denise.

I know that laugh, that voice screaming hateful slurs in my mind.

Having been near the cake, waiting for a slice, I reach out and grab the icing-coated weapon and lunge toward Julian, his eyes widening in both confusion and fear as I madly scream, going straight for his throat with the large knife.

Except it's not me. Denise is in control, using my body to do her vengeful bidding.

Julian grabs my wrists, holding them away from him, pushing me away, trying not to hurt me.

"Ivy!" he shouts. "The hell?!"

A menacing laugh crawls up my throat: "Ivy's gone."

Julian's eyes widen further as he stares back at me. "Denise?!"

"She's mine now, bitch!" Screaming now, lunging still: "And so are you!"

I'm screaming myself, but no one can hear. *Julian! Help! I can't stop her!*

"Ivy?" Julian grunts, still trying to hold Denise off. Relief washes over his features. "I know you're in there. Hold on!" He wrestles with Denise's spirit, both of us falling to the floor with Julian on top of me, holding my wrists down against the cold, hard marble. "Let her go, dammit!"

"Never!" Denise shouts, still wriggling under Julian's weight.

Suddenly I'm doused with something cold and wet, straight in my face. Denise screams as the weight is lifted from me, setting me free, her spirit emerging from my form in a swirling dark cloud, her figure soon disappearing through the ceiling.

The lights flicker back on, and the coldness and heaviness of dread leaves us.

Julian hesitantly releases my wrists, his worried eyes searching mine. "Ivy?"

"It's me," I say, wiping at my eyes, mascara smudges on the back of my hand now. "What... what happened? H-how...?"

"Holy water," Velda announces, holding up the half-empty bottle. "Came in handy sooner than I thought."

"Did... did we just get attacked by a ghost?!" someone asks.

Velda looks at the ceiling where Denise disappeared. "The veil between dimensions is open. We'll need to protect ourselves from future attacks and possessions."

"How?" Julian asks, lifting me to my feet, holding me close against his chest.

Velda looks at him. "My suggestion? Use crystals, like Black Obsidian. Spirits hate such natural elements."

Julian asks: "Black Obsidian?"

"Or Black Tourmaline."

"What do we do with 'em?" he asks.

She shrugs. "Wear it in jewelry, keep a crystal in your pocket..."

"That's it?" I ask.

"You can also cleanse your homes with burning sage. Or get a sage candle from my shop. Same thing... except the candle smells better."

Someone laughs: "You fuckin' with us? This all a hoax?"

Velda turns to find a vampire looking at her like she must be joking, his hands on his hips, a grin on his lips.

"I never joke about evil," she responds, facing us again next. She reaches out and touches my shoulder, noticing I'm shaking. She lowers her voice, the sound soothing: "It'll be okay, Ivy. I won't let her hurt you again." She looks around the room, her eyes settling on Landon's, who's come to stand next to her. "None of you."

I hold Julian tighter, closing my eyes, taking deep breaths, trying to control the fear that's sent my heart into a panicked frenzy of quickened beats.

Velda removes her hand from my shoulder and stands straighter. "I'll fix this. It's my fault the demon is loose, that all the souls its collected can now pass between dimensions with ease."

"Wait...," Julian objects. "You sayin' that demon collected Denise's soul?"

Velda eyes Julian curiously. "Yes, why?"

"Well... I... killed her." Velda's eyes widen in surprise hearing his confession. He holds me tighter. "She didn't give me much of a choice." His voice becomes angry: "She threatened Ivy. Threatened me. Must be why she came here tonight... to finish the job."

She looks between us. "As I've told you before – this demon is drawn to terror. It must've snatched her soul when you killed her."

"She didn't seem afraid to me," he mutters.

"I was," I admit. "I was terrified that day."

Velda gives me a sympathetic look. "I promise I *will* end that demon and set the captured souls free. I'll make things right." Her jaw clenches. "If it's the last thing I ever do."

Don't miss out!

Visit the website below and you can sign up to receive emails whenever K.R. Cook publishes a new book. There's no charge and no obligation.

https://books2read.com/r/B-A-QKDM-MIMXB

BOOKS 2 READ

Connecting independent readers to independent writers.

Did you love *Undertaken and Undone*? Then you should read
Unleashed and Undone[1] by K.R. Cook!

[2]

Velda Everspark is a talented witch who owns her own apothecary
and metaphysical shop in a city crawling with vamps. After her friend
Mindy is murdered by the same serial killer vamp who's been targeting
blondes since Undead & Undone, Velda takes matters into her own
hands in finding and destroying the murderous menace, even resorting
to using dark magick to do so. Unfortunately, she accidentally
unleashes a soul-collecting demon, weakening the very Hell dimension
it comes from in the process, allowing the spirits it'd collected to walk
freely among the living.

Landon Reeves, a werewolf seeking a pack, shows up just in time to
find his mate and witness her descent into vengeful madness. Though

---

1. https://books2read.com/u/mdjOpR

2. https://books2read.com/u/mdjOpR

chaos ensues, Landon fights to save Velda and protect her, even from herself. Sprinkle in some vengeful spirits, a dash of terrifying premonitions, and an impending apocalypse on the horizon, romance definitely isn't on Velda's to-do list. Despite these obstacles, neither can deny the passion and desire that burns brilliantly between them, even when Landon's ex, one of the spirits unleashed from the Hell dimension, targets and torments his new beau.

Will Velda destroy the demon and set the stolen souls it's collected free so they may find peace on the other side? Can she prevent the apocalypse and save the world? One thing's for certain: She can't do any of it alone. Lucky for her, she has a mate hellbent on protecting her, a new pack who has her back, and a strong-willed younger sister who possesses her own set of magical abilities.

Read more at https://www.authorkrcook.com/.

Also by K.R. Cook

Submerged Series
Submerged
Unleashed
Overcoming

Undone Series
Undead and Undone
Untamed and Undone
Undertaken and Undone
Unleashed and Undone
Undeniable and Undone

Watch for more at https://www.authorkrcook.com/.

About the Author

K.R. Cook is a romance author residing in Texas with her husband and their three beautiful dogs. When she isn't creating captivating fictional worlds and love stories, she's spending time with family, plotting her next book, engaging with other readers and writers, and creating social media content. Fall is her favorite season - when the air turns crisp and magical, you'll catch her enjoying a hot double spice chai tea and putting sweaters on her pups (don't worry, they love it).

For more information on books, visit her website and subscribe at authorkrcook.com.

Read more at https://www.authorkrcook.com/.